The Seeing Eye

by Samuel Hayes Sherwood

ISBN 978-1-7323109-0-2

This is a work of fiction. The characters are both actual and fictitious. With the exception of verified historical events and persons, all incidents, descriptions, dialogue and opinions expressed are the products of the author's imagination and are not to be construed as real.

Published by

SHERWOOD
PRESS

yetnotibutchrist.com

DEDICATION

First and foremost to the author and finisher of our faith, Jesus Christ, who saw this as a completed work before any ink was laid to paper.

To my wife, Deborah, who instilled the thrill of reading and literature in young hearts for over thirty years.

To my daughters, Susan Dunfee and Samantha Bononno, our gifts from God.

THE

SEEING

EYE

SAMUEL HAYES SHERWOOD

SHERWOOD
PRESS

I

THEY SAY, *"red sky at night, sailor's delight; red sky in morning, sailor's warning."* The dark clouds of November paid no homage to the warning part as they assembled for winter's first kiss.

Inside the dimly lit hallway, the chill was no less. Like two unwilling gladiators, they faced off, each waiting for the other to cast the first blow.

David McKinley looked him all over. He held out his hand breaking the standoff.

The boy removed the sunglasses and handed them over.

The teacher cringed. "What happened, Carl?" he asked.

"Door," he replied stoically.

Right. David's cheeks turned a darker shade of pink at the boy's veiled answer. He weighed the resoluteness of his student's face against more pressing cares. Another minute of silent reverie passed as they both wished the moment to go away. *I just don't need this right now*, thought the teacher.

"There seem to be a lot of hazards in that house of yours," he said yielding to his opponent.

Carl made no response.

"OK, take your seat." He handed him back his sunglasses. "Here. You may need these."

The classroom banter was quickly snuffed out like a candle as the teacher in professorial tweed entered and marched toward the front of the room to finish writing on the board. As Carl took his seat in the back, the boys turned their heads away. A few girls shared their horror with visceral squeals. One threatening look from the teacher silenced everyone. All their shiny faces focused on the board.

"OK, you writer wannabes," said Mr. McKinley. "You see the sentence on the board."

It read, "Michael sat down in the middle of the road and began to cry."

"Start writing. You have six minutes." David started the timer and sat down.

The class stared at the board with confused puppy dog looks as if they were asked to decode a secret message from outer space. Andy Morris raised his hand.

"Yes, Mr. Morris," said Mr. McKinley.

"Write what?" he asked. The rest of the class distanced themselves from their ignorant classmate by putting their noses to the paper, but their ears were watching intently.

"Whatever you want, Mr. Morris," he replied with a look that confirmed to everyone that, yes, there are stupid questions. "It's all about imagination. Be creative. Just start writing."

The blank sheet of paper in front of the red headed rotund student was like looking into a mirror.

Some started writing their names on the header in slow motion hoping that would provide enough time for an idea to come from above. Others gnarled the end of their pens waiting for an epiphany that, should it come, would frighten them as much as their teacher. Some looked for inspiration out the window. The swirling flurries looked like . . . well, swirling flurries. It didn't come. Nevertheless, one by one, the teacher watched their eyes light up like an electronic game board as they began to lay ink to paper.

Then there was Carl. For him there was no delay. He was the only one off the blocks instantly. His hand was moving furiously as if his story was already written and six minutes was nowhere sufficient to hear it out. David was concerned. His pen was bearing down so hard on the paper, he assumed the paper would be in shreds or there would be an indelible copy carved on the wooden desk.

The alarm went off. The class lifted their heads in relief only to groan as a new sentence appeared on the board—"On the following Friday, we packed our bags and planned our escape."

"Keep writing," he instructed. Andy Morris's face begged for more enlightenment. "Tie the two sentences together in the same story, Andy. Six more minutes and I will give you another transitional sentence."

Some paused long enough to forge a connection between the two seemingly random phrases. To others, the chasm to bridge was no less infinite than the east is from the west. The pen biters looked more like dumbfounded cattle chewing their cuds. But Carl's hand never stopped moving. He glanced up at the new sentence like it of course made sense and kept going without taking a breath.

The ringing period bell was drowned out by sighs of relief. Backpacks and cellphones were grabbed with the hope of escaping with their stories, but that foolish thought quickly turned to muffled groans.

"Easy. Hold on," Mr. McKinley raising his voice above the noise. "Bring your papers down front on your way out."

They indexed down front with the enthusiasm of meeting a Catholic nun holding a wooden ruler in her hand. Carl's six foot head could be seen bobbing above the rest, bringing up the rear. He looked straight ahead with no eye contact as if marching to an execution. A few girls tried to flirt some empathy only to bounce off his impenetrable force field. But David saw cracks in that armor as the boy handed in his paper. Carl turned with a little less certainty, slowly making his way out with the energy of a prize fighter who was left standing after twelve rounds, but that was about all.

David McKinley watched the enigmatic boy walk away. The faded jeans he wore everyday were creased to a frayed knife edge by uncounted meetings with a flat iron. He was sure he had seen that same sweater many days in a row. *That boy had shown so much promise a year ago*, he thought. *Now it was hit or miss. What's going on?*

He looked wearily at the pile of writing he would have to read that weekend and markup. The one on top grabbed his attention. It was Carl's. "Michael sat down in the middle of the road and began to cry, *not because he had killed him, but because he hadn't killed him sooner.*"

What is this all about? thought David as he eased himself carefully into his wobbly swivel chair and began to read more. When he came to the non sequitur line, it read, "On the following Friday, we packed our bags and planned our escape, *but it was too late. We should have left that Friday and not waited. Then it wouldn't have happened.*"

He kept reading it over and over until he noticed a full class was staring him in the face. *What do I do with this now?* He wondered. *School counselor? I don't need this right now . . . especially now.* He put Carl's paper on the bottom of the stack and began writing on the board.

§§§

The only minute more eternal than the one before the last bell of the day was the minute before the lunch bell. Students launched out of their seats so fast drawing into question whether the speed of sound had been correctly calculated. But despite their abilities to break the sound barrier, there was one immutable low tech law they could not break. The same unnamed law that governs the grains of sand dripping from an hourglass applied to them. They had to exit one at a time.

David was not in so much of a hurry. He slunk in his chair and watched all that youthful energy drain from the room. *One more morning under the belt. One more afternoon to get through.* And it was his birthday. *If they make a fuss . . . and I know who . . .* He considered eating his baloney sandwich right there. *Mary would jump on me for being antisocial,* he thought as he shouldered his beat up leather satchel and started trudging toward the teacher's lounge. *And then they'll talk the same old stuff like a worn out record. There has to be something more exciting than the weather. Or Common Core. Hey, it's Maine. It's November. What do you expect? Don't like it? Move to Florida. Don't like Common Core? Move to Russia!*

David opened the door. His ill-fated prophesy did not let him down, nor did it waste any time. *Oh no, he's really going to do it.* It was too late.

Howard Bates stood front and center with a lopsided chocolate cake sporting a lonely candle, clearly a failed experiment from Mrs. Merkle's freshman home ec class.

"Happy Birthday, neighbor," said Howie leading the cheer while his backup band of colleagues clapped with about the same excitement as pulling lunchroom duty.

I'm not your neighbor, Howie. David forced a slight nod. "Thank you," he said as he bee lined to his table in hopes of avoiding any further festivities. But that was not to be so.

No. Howie conducted a short arrangement of Happy Birthday swinging the cake around like a baton. David's eyes tracked the oscillating cake waiting for it plop on the floor but somehow even the candle stayed lit.

And I thought just his speaking voice was irritating, thought David. "Thank you, everyone," David repeated and sat down, again hoping to stay any further attention. But that was not to be so either. Howard shadowed him to his table and started slicing up the cake on paper plates. Then he handed David an extra-large piece and sat down beside him. *I'm sure this will be served with a generous side of self-righteousness,* thought David.

David looked at his cake and then his baloney sandwich.

"Not bad, neighbor," joked Howie as he wiped chocolate frosting off his frumpy mustache. "Try some."

David continued to ignore him.

"Hey, what's the matter? Forty is the new thirty, these days," he said leaning closer to David who automatically pulled back as if magnetically repulsed.

"Right," murmured David. *Like that's my problem. And forty is forty, you idiot.* He closed his eyes and prayed that Howie would go away. It didn't work. Let down again. He pulled out his baloney sandwich and started munching, a hint that also went unheeded.

"David," Howie started, "I know you have some serious issues right now."

Oh, here we go.

"We have Mary on the prayer list."

Good job, Howie. It's not working.

"Yes, we pray for her every week. I was discussing this with the pastor. He thought it would be nice if we could stop by and pray with you and Mary."

Now that should really light a fire under God.

"I know you come from a family of faith . . ."

David started to grind his teeth. *Seriously. What do you know about me, you . . .*

". . . and there is power in prayer. Whatever we ask in Jesus' name, he will do."

Does he really believe this stuff? Power in prayer? Jesus has left the building you moron. The tips of David's ears were turning pink, a sign that only Mary knew was a wise time to stop. Howard didn't.

"I know it's hard for us to wrap our mind around, but the Bible says that all things work together for good to those who love God."

"Really?" whispered David through his teeth. His eyes were rolling around in his head as if he were about to be possessed. He turned toward his comforter and wondered what fantasy world he was living in. *All good, huh? I'll pray you get some of that goodness. Maybe some of us aren't such great lovers of God as you!* His ears were now a light shade of red.

"Look, we have a new pastor. He's really good. This Sunday he is going to preach a great sermon on faith and how God gives

back a hundred fold if we just believe. You know the Bible says
to count it all joy . . ."

The tips of David's ears looked like ripe red peppers. The
spring Howard had been ignorantly winding had created enough
energy to lacerate anyone within the walls of Woodspring High
School and it was about to snap.

Starting in a slow, tight voice, he started to unwind. "You
know, Howie . . . If you parrot one more of those memorized
scriptures in my face, you'll be eating this chocolate cake
through your nose."

"What?" Howie arched back in fear as David looked like his
head was about to rotate all the way around on his shoulders. "I .
. . I was just trying to help . . .," he stuttered.

"Help . . . help?" mimicked David as his scorning voice
quickly crescendoed to a volume filling the room. "Surely, you
jest. Just who do you think you are? Helping with all this
mumbo jumbo from some book of fables? You self-righteous . . .
maybe you need to get a hold on real life. All things are not good,
Howie. Do you know that? Maybe it's because everything is
going so well for you that you are so ignorant. Isn't that what you
all say? 'God is good?' Until your world comes falling apart. Joy,
you say? Well I should have a hell of a lot of it. Oh jubilation. I
can't stand it. My wife is lying in bed ready to flat line any
moment. Oh joy, joy, joy . . ." he spurned. "If I get much more
joy, I just won't be able to handle it all. Spare me all that fake
concern. I don't need it. I can take care of my own problems
without your help. And I've heard all about that great preacher
of yours. It sounds like I couldn't afford to join up. Why don't
you tell that church of yours to take care of its own and leave me
alone. Spread that joy somewhere else. If you are so hell-bent on
helping, how about that boy this morning? Carl. Isn't he a
member of your holy, God fearing church? Maybe you ought to
worry less about saving my soul and work on doing something
real, saving the flesh. Looks like he might be getting more joy
than he wants too. Maybe you could peddle this crap to him."

David stood up and looked around. Everyone's heads were
turned. Their mouths were wide open with half chewed food as if
they had just witnessed a non-fatal murder. His head looked like
it was ready to spontaneously combust.

"Sorry," he muttered. He grabbed the other half of his
baloney sandwich and slammed it in the trash can on the way
out.

II

MRS. BECKETT exchanged the Macy's webpage for weather.com. Record cold expected tonight, it said. Not much accumulation, maybe one to two inches. Her glasses hung low on her nose as she confirmed the forecast out the window. It was like looking at a life size snow globe. Thick flurries swirled around the parking lot lights like thousands of mosquitoes being attracted to an icy death. Red taillights disappeared into the mist. The few remaining cars looked like white buffalos stuck in frozen tundra.

Her eyes alternated between the clock and her sole customer on this Friday afternoon. Carl was a frequent visitor to the library while waiting for the bus, but it was 4:30, it was as dark as midnight, and time for everyone to go home.

The headlights of the last late bus emerged off the highway and circled to the pickup point. Boys with unzipped varsity jackets and no hats pushed up the open bus door. Girls bundled up like fashionable Eskimos tested the existence of any remaining chivalry, patiently waiting a turn to board. Carl moved to the next algebra problem.

Mrs. Beckett watched the bus close its doors and looked over at Carl. "Carl, aren't you going to miss your bus?" she asked.

"No, ma'am," he replied, picking up his head for a second before dropping it back into his work. "My bus left thirty minutes ago."

"It's getting pretty nasty out there. I guess you have a ride?" she asked rhetorically starting to shut down her computer and clear off her desk.

"Yes, ma'am," he said.

Mrs. Beckett continued her routine of shutting up the library in a pronounced way that left little doubt of her intentions. Carl kept working, showing no inclination to stop what he was doing. Finally she pulled her keys out of her drawer and clanged them on the desk and reached for her coat signaling last call. Carl surrendered with a sigh. He closed his book and slipped everything into his backpack.

Mrs. Beckett stood holding the door with her keys in hand. As Carl passed, she looked incuriously at his swollen face which by now was old news. She locked the door and turned left toward the lobby door. "Good night," whispered Carl, as he turned right toward his locker. He exchanged his backpack for a thin brown leather jacket. He zipped it up, turned his collar to the wind, and stepped out into the cold like a man committed to his fate. As he walked off school property, Mrs. Beckett's car almost clipped him. Her nose was pushed up in the little hand hole clearing on the windshield while her wipers were furiously doing battle with the snowflakes.

Walking five miles in a freezing whiteout would have given anyone else pause, but Carl gave no thought to what was before him. He just marched. The icy blasts of wind wasted no time embracing its victim who in turn embraced it back just as heartedly. It felt so good, the cold. He felt alive. For a short time there was something more powerful than the pain he was feeling. Something able to subdue it, swallow it up, and numb all the hurt and anger that consumed him. Cars sped by, their taillights quickly vanishing in a violent whirlwind of snow. He wished one of those whirlwinds could lift him up and take him somewhere else . . . anywhere else. One car slowed and tapped its brake lights like it was going to stop, but kept going. It looked vaguely familiar.

Each car that went by enveloped him in a cloud of white powder. It felt like he was making his way along some fallen ethereal world of cold and darkness. *Not much different than the real world*, he thought. After an hour, the sweet numbness that had soothed his soul had thoroughly numbed the flesh. He started to lose feeling in his hands and feet. His only line of defense was the thick wool sweater his mother had knitted, the last thing he remembered her giving him. His hands alternated between cupping his ears and thawing them in his pockets until they wouldn't thaw anymore. He started walking stiff legged like the living dead.

Finally, he came to the dirt side road that led up to Jumbo's cabin. He started up the logging road, his thoughts now preoccupied with visions of a warm wood stove and a true friend. He had not decided whether or not he would go home that night. He looked at his watch. The only safe time was when he was passed out drunk. The passing out was a given; the timing not so much.

The dim yellow cabin light, barely visible through the trees, was to Carl like a brilliant lighthouse beacon leading him to safety. As he rounded that last bend, he could see Jumbo's small rusted bulldozer pulled in under the side canopy. He hadn't been home long. Fresh tracks led from the woods. Snowflakes were still melting on the engine canopy.

Jumbo, christened Keme Lightfoot, lived in this cabin with his older brother, Ben. They were Micmacs. Carl and Jumbo began their friendship in the third grade. Both being from the other side of the tracks made them a common target. Carl held his own as best he could. If he turned sideways, there wasn't much to hit, but that wasn't much of a defense. Jumbo, on the other hand, was two years older having been held back twice. He was shorter but almost as wide as he was tall. That included no fat. They dared to call him Indian Bob SquarePants when out of earshot. Later it was fearfully the Red Incredible Hulk. By the time he entered Junior High he was called more deferentially Jumbo. That stuck. He even kind of liked it.

The synergistic combo of brains and brawn bought safe passage through elementary and junior high. Thanks to Carl's tutoring, Jumbo elevated himself to a higher than average academic status. But the schools were not wont to expending much energy on those profiled to rise no higher than lumberjack status. Despite Carl and his mother begging him to keep going, Jumbo called it quits after the eighth grade. He was going to work. He bought a small dozer and started hauling logs out of the woods. The system felled one more victim.

Carl was afraid his fists would shatter like glass so he knocked as loudly on the wooden door as he could with his elbows. The few seconds felt like minutes before a big round brown face opened the door. For another second Jumbo stared at him in disbelief as if he were looking at the first and only frozen skinny Yeti to ever appear on someone's doorstep. Then he stiffened with anger at the sight of Carl's face. He shook his head.

"Again? Get in here, Kemosabe, you fool," he grunted yanking him in and quickly slamming the door. "What in the world are you doing?"

Carl tried to smile, but he couldn't. He tried to form some words, but his skill as a ventriloquist was revealed to be . . . nonexistent. His utterances sounded more like a heretofore never discovered ancient language. He stared at the wood stove starting to radiate heat from the center of the room like someone in love.

"Easy, buddy," Jumbo said helping him off with his jacket and setting him on the couch. "I'll have this fired up in no time. Just got in. Let's get these boots off."

Jumbo pulled them off and shook his head one more time. "Who in Maine doesn't have insulated boots? Send these goofy things back to Bean and get some real boots."

Jumbo stoked the fire and added two more sticks of wood. Carl tried to move his feet closer to the heat.

"Wait a minute," said Jumbo pulling his socks off. "Feel anything?"

Carl shook his head.

"Just wait." Jumbo grabbed a basin and filled it with water. "Stick your feet in this first," he instructed, setting it down in front of him.

The cold water felt warm to his feet. Carl leaned his head back starting to relax for the first time today. There was even a subliminal look of satisfaction. It might have taken extra rounds, but he felt like he was finally dancing in the winner's circle.

"Tell me," Jumbo asked, "are you nuts?"

"Pwobabwe," he replied.

"Right. You're starting to make sense now." Jumbo shook his head. "Looks like he did a J–O–B on you this time," he said as he walked over and shoved another stick of wood in the stove and closed it up.

"Don feel a ting," said Carl.

Jumbo turned and looked at his pathetic friend trying to laugh. He couldn't help but expose a row of white teeth with one black hole in the front, the consequence of accepting a dare to open a bottle of beer with his mouth. "I'll bet you don't."

It didn't take long to heat up the small cabin of two rooms and a loft. His brother had the one bedroom while Jumbo slept above it. The wood stove was the center piece. There was one couch which was often Carl's bed, two worn out overstuffed chairs, a rickety kitchen table and matching chairs, and an old TV set with tin foiled rabbit ears. "But it has indoor plumbing," Jumbo would joke proudly. It was home.

"Beer? Looks like you need one," asked Jumbo opening the fridge.

"Kaawfeee," mumbled Carl.

"What?"

Carl worked a few calisthenics with his mouth before trying again. "Coffee," he replied. He could finally feel the warmth start to penetrate upward through his bones.

"Yeah, right. Bad idea." Jumbo put a kettle of water on the stove.

"Where's Ben?"

Jumbo just looked at him. "Pay day."

"Right."

The sink was full of dirty dishes and the trash can was full of beer and Dinty Moore cans. Jumbo washed a pot out in the sink, opened two new cans of beef stew and set it on the stove along with some leftover cornbread.

"We'll feast tonight," he said with thumbs up.

The tea kettle started a faint whistle. He opened a bottle of Folgers Instant Coffee and tapped a generous ration into a cup. He handed the steaming coffee to Carl and sat down beside him.

Jumbo took a closer look at the side of Carl's face. "Wanta talk about it?" he asked.

Carl looked over at his friend. "Not really. Not much to say."

"That sonofa . . . ," Jumbo started. "Doesn't look like a fist did that."

Carl sipped his coffee in silence. He stared at the TV in front of him as if it were replaying the sorry episode. The reflection of his face in the black screen did no justice to the real hurt.

"How long are you going to put up with this?" Jumbo said in a poor attempt to contain his vicarious anger. "Dad or no dad, I'd put a quick end to it. I managed without one. Hey, and look at how I turned out," he said holding his hands in the air and making a goofy face, "an entrepreneur at eighteen."

Carl knew what Jumbo meant. It was a thought that seemed to surface more and more with less and less repugnance. *Before he kills me*, he thought.

"Look, man. I wouldn't be able to spell entrepreneur without you. Whatever you need, I'm here."

"I know," he replied. *I know.*

So, what are you going to do?" asked Jumbo.

"I don't know. I'm sixteen now. I guess that gives me some rights."

"You know you can come live here. Ben would have no problem with that."

"I thought that was what I was doing," Carl said.

"Pretty close. It's an open invitation."

"Well, tip toeing around him isn't working. Sooner or later there is always a confrontation. And I think he's starting to get scared of me which makes him all the more unstable. I'm at least his size now. I just don't have anyone to talk to about it."

"Tell me about it."

"I may have to take you up on your offer," Carl said. "Not many options. I'll take the guest room." He gurgled a laugh.

"You mean what you're sitting on? Then it's settled."

Jumbo pulled the bubbling stew and cornbread off the stove and set it on the table. He washed out some silverware and bowls. "We'll get fancy and celebrate," he said dumping the stew into the bowls. He reached over and turned on the TV.

"Wow. A proper dinner, and with a movie no less," joked Carl pulling up a chair.

"Good to hear you laugh, friend," said Jumbo.

"It hurts."

A snowy picture flickered on the screen. Static garbled the words as the six o'clock news came on. Jumbo fumbled with the rabbit ears and smoothed out the tinfoil. "This storm, I guess," he said. "Happens every time." The best he could get was a foggy rendition of a police mug shot of a bare chested man just as it left the screen. The sound was in and out.

"That guy looks familiar," said Carl leaning closer to the screen.

"A local man was arrested late this afternoon for assaulting a police officer," said the anchor. "His name is Ke**** C**k of Wood*****, Maine. Police say he is also a Person of Interest in an unspecified investigation. Police have issued search warrants for his house."

The phone rang. Jumbo listened intently to whomever was on the other end as Carl strained to hear more and continued to refine the picture and sound. Finally Jumbo hung up.

"Who was that?" Carl asked.

"Ben," Jumbo replied. "He called from the Blue Ox Bar and Grill."

"Oh," Carl replied as he gave up on his TV repair. "What's he up to?"

"Let's just say you don't have to worry about going home tonight."

"Why is that?"

"That's your old man on TV, buddy. He was just arrested."

"For assaulting a police officer?"

Jumbo hesitated. "That's what they say. The rumor is murder."

Carl's face lost all expression. "Murder. Murder of whom?" But it was rhetorical. He knew. Jumbo knew.

III

DAVID MCKINLEY was a writer. He was no scientist or mathematician. He didn't know much about the theory of relativity. But one thing he had come to believe was that time did move at different speeds. Not to take anything away from the genius of Albert Einstein, but country folk figured it out long before he was born. His mother summed it up quite simply: *"A watched pot never boils."* He hated it when she was right.

His freshman English class was hunkered down over a grammar exam. The clock stood still. A pile of papers from the morning's creative writing class lay in front of him. He knew he should grade them before he left. There would be no time over the weekend. Normally it would be an enjoyable task, but tonight it was just one more heavy weight to bear. He couldn't concentrate. His mind was preoccupied with getting home to Mary, but more on the fool he had made of himself. All afternoon, he bare knuckle bloodied himself up but he was still short on sufficient penance. He was ashamed to make eye contact with staff or students. Every whisper turned his head. That professional armor he thought he had hammered out to perfection was found not so perfect . . . exposed . . . cracked . . . a fraud.

How did I let that self-righteous, self-called prig get to me? he thought, continuing his self-emasculation. *I, of all people, should be the world's greatest at letting that stuff roll off. I've heard it all before. I grew up with it. Boy, did I grow up with it. I've been beat with it, dunked in it, had my nose rubbed in it. Ignorance can't be corrected. By definition they have no clue they're ignorant. They're brainwashed. You can't tell them anything. There is no way a "good" God, a God of love, can allow the things he does. Why couldn't I just smile and nod. Idiot. Let it go. How did I let my buttons get pushed this time?*

And so he continued with his rambling manifesto never to be shared until the class bell rang. Students marched down front with long faces and their tests. He still had a planning period to fill. *I need to do something.* Heaving a great sigh, he grabbed a red pen and that stack of papers that had been staring at him all day and got to work. *Maybe this will get my mind straight,* he thought.

He worked the pile down to the last one, Carl's. He read it and then read it again. Each time he was more shocked. It wasn't just that it was written as well as any short story he had ever seen from a student; no, it was more than the mere words. It was the feelings they evoked like a siren drawing its reader unknowingly to a palpable place that was passionate . . . true . . . but so dark. Each page reached up and grabbed you by the throat and shook you. *But, what's going on with this boy that he writes stuff like this?* He left only one red mark on this paper—A+.

He looked up at the clock. *Guess there is something to that relativity stuff.* Time had apparently moved faster when he wasn't looking. It was already five o'clock. He had thirty minutes to get home. His was the last car in the parking lot. Stuffing everything into his satchel, he grabbed his coat and started for the lobby. Stepping outside was like being tasered. This Siberian Express would not be mocked. He quickly pulled up his collar, managed to fasten a couple buttons and then fumbled for his gloves. Snowflakes camouflaged themselves in his salt and pepper hair as he ran to the car trying his best not to slip. His gloved hand shook as he felt for the ignition slot and turned the key. He revved up the defroster and made one more sprint outside the car to scrape the windshield. He got back in and waited about thirty seconds. *Man, it will take forever to make a dent with this defroster,* he thought, taking his glove and clearing a peep hole just large enough to see. *Can't wait.* With his face up close to the windshield, David navigated slowly out of the parking lot onto the main road.

Accumulation wasn't much, but the flying snow had produced almost whiteout conditions. The traffic was moving no more than thirty five miles an hour. David couldn't pass. A couple miles down the road his headlights bounced off what looked like an apparition shrouded in a halo of white slowly walking along the shoulder. "Who is that," he said to himself, "walking along the road trying to get hit?" He turned his head to see as he came alongside. *Is that Carl?* He started to slow down but the clock on the dash said no. *Carl is smarter than that.* He sped up.

Dave pulled into his driveway. The Toyota Prius belonging to Ann was still there. The old garage door greeted him with its gregarious smile, not uncoincidentally matching the shape of his old Buick's rear bumper. Tonight it had frosted lips.

Remembering how upset Mary was when it happened always seemed to lance some of the poison out of him. Dave laughed it off and told her it added character to an otherwise boring rancher. He did wish he could afford to fix it, but that was the last of his worries. He was buried with enough bills coming from so many different directions; it would challenge the mightiest forensic accountant to sort it out. Doctors. Hospitals. Clinics. Labs. Medical companies he wasn't sure even existed. It was endless.

The only exception was Ann Delaney, a private RN who showed up at the door one day after Mary was discharged from the hospital, or as David put it, dumped out on the street. If Ann hadn't shown up, he had no idea what he would have done. She had a hospital bed and monitoring equipment delivered. She took care of Mary weekdays and trained David on how to use all the equipment as well as the AED when she wasn't there. He never would have conceived his insurance would cover it. His only experience so far was they were nothing less than a greedy sociopathic oligarchy sucking as much blood out of its victims as it could without actually killing them. But he never received a bill. He never asked why.

But he also knew even that wouldn't be enough. David pulled his collar to the wind and ran into the house slamming the cold out behind him. He hung his coat on the rack and made his way to the dining room. There was a time when he hated hospitals with their sterile smells. The monotonous blips and chirps felt more like Chinese water torture. Now they were welcoming sounds that signaled all is good. Red and green LEDs flickered in the dimly lit room giving it the aura of a clandestine hospital operation.

"Hi, David," Ann said quietly getting up from her bedside chair and moving to the kitchen. "She just dozed off. I understand birthday wishes are in order?"

"Hi, Ann," he replied looking in at his wife. "Yeah, thanks, but I pretty much had all the celebration I can take today. How is she doing?"

"No, change. She's been resting very well. We had a good day. I just fed her some chicken soup. She should be OK through the night."

"Thanks," he said sitting down. "Any instructions?"

"Not really. You know what to do. If something happens, hit the alarm for the EMT's. The AED is charged. There isn't anything much we can do differently. Sorry."

Dave looked up at her with the same eyes she had seen many times begging an answer to a question he didn't dare ask—how much longer?

"Have faith, David. She sure does," Ann replied wishing she could sugar coat it. "I can tell you I have never been so blessed in my life knowing such a person as your wife. She has such assurance that no matter what happens, God is in control and it will work out according to His will and His glory. The only thing she prays for everyday is that you can share in that assurance."

Right, he thought, *God's will again. Allah's will. Somebody's will. What about my will? What will I do without her? She's all I have.* He offered no resistance as an all too familiar bell jar of depression descended.

"I know," he said. "There is no one like her. She has always had the faith. She is the bravest person I know."

"I can hear you," said Mary from the makeshift hospital room.

"Sorry, Hon," said Dave leaning over and kissing her on the cheek. "Didn't mean to wake you."

"You didn't. And I'm not brave, David," she said. "I'm no braver than anyone else. I just know in my heart of hearts that everything will be all right."

"So you keep telling me," he said holding her hand. *I love you, even if you don't make sense.*

"Ann, you will have to be careful out there," he said. "It's treacherous."

"I know. Been watching the weather all day," she said reaching for her coat. "The good news is it will warm back up in a couple days."

Dave helped her with her coat and ran out to clean the snow off her car. The dry flakes brushed off easily. He came back in and stomped his feet in the mud room.

"Mary," he yelled, "I'm going to grab something out of the fridge. Didn't have much lunch today." The knot in his gut had nothing to do with hunger.

"OK," she said. "There should be some leftover spaghetti. Sorry I couldn't make you a birthday cake."

"Don't worry. I had enough cake today to last a while." *Boy, did I.*

Dave stood in in front of the refrigerator vacillating between the spaghetti and the meatloaf. The great decision was delayed by a ringing phone. *Who is that? Oh great. Debbie. That's all I need. Another weight to bear. What does she want now?*

"Hello," he answered as toneless as one would answering a robocall.

"Happy birthday, baby brother," came a singsong voice. She sounded like she was in a tunnel.

Apparently couldn't wait to get home and make a proper call. The baby brother joke from his baby sister was always annoying. *Who got who through college? Who wrote your papers when you were pressed? Who continued to give while his sister got rich and never gave anything back in return, let alone respect?*

"Yeah, Sis . . . baby brother," he replied.

"Sorry, Dave," she said. "I was just teasing. This is the big four–o. You don't sound too excited."

"Oh, I'm excited. One more year closer to the end."

"Wow, what a downer, brother. Look, I know things are tough right now. How is Mary doing?"

"Well, how do you think she is?" he replied, his voice already getting louder. "I've been waiting for the Pope or the second coming, but you know what? They aren't coming. So you figure it out."

"David, David," cried Mary hoarsely. "Calm down. That is your sister."

Her words were drowned out in his escalating fury.

"What can I do to help?" she asked. "I'm afraid for you. You are wound so tight. Look, I can take off a few days and fly up there."

"You know, Sis, it's a little too late for help now. There was a time, but you were nowhere to be found."

"What do you mean?" she asked. "I've always been there for you."

"What?" he screamed. This time he didn't bother to ramp up to a furor. He just blew with a quake that would make Mt. St. Helens proud.

"David . . . David," cried Mary. "Stop it. What is the matter with you?" The chirps started getting closer and fainter.

"When have you ever been there for me or anyone but yourself? Where were you when we were about bankrupt? When we were running all over the country going crazy with doctors and hospitals? Are you serious? You have been nothing but selfish from the time you were a kid to when Mom died and then you kept that miserable little inheritance for yourself. And you sit down there in Florida on the water, with a big boat, and BMWs . . ."

"Now wait a minute, there wasn't enough money from that inheritance to put her in the ground," Debbie interjected.

"No, you wait a minute," he yelled cutting her off. The voice from the other room was getting weaker, the chirps more frequent. "I think it's time for you to be totally on your own. I can't help you anymore."

"You can't help me?" she cried.

"Yes, I have enough load to bear. I don't need you. I'm going to have to cut you off."

"Cut me off? What in the world is that supposed to mean?"

"It means we're through. I've done all I can for you. I've got my own problems to take care of."

The line was silent. "I'll pray for you, David," she said calmly.

"Pray for me? Pray for me?" He was now screaming into the mouthpiece. "I wish all of you would take those prayers and . . ."

He heard a *thunk*. The line went dead. "Go ahead and hang up," he yelled into a deaf line. "Goodbye." He banged the receiver down on the cradle.

He sat down in the kitchen unable to cool down. He looked around. Something had changed. It was eerie. "What's going on?" he said getting up. "Where are the chirps? What's that sound?"

He scrambled to the dining room. There lay Mary motionless. Her face was turning blue. The heart monitor eked out a sickening monotone. The screen over the bed had flat lined. He panicked. "What have I done?" He grabbed the defibrillator and yelled to God or anyone who would listen, "Clear!"

IV

IT IS said that the darkest hour is just before dawn. Carl lay sleepless on the couch certain that an even darker hour than that lay before him. The lonely wind whistled through the pines like a siren calling for its soul mate. *I hear you,* he answered silently. As if taking that as an invitation, the wind slipped its icy tentacles through the drafty windows and the thin covers. Rejecting the overture, he got up and put two more sticks of wood in the stove. He could hear Jumbo snoring from the loft. He pulled a chair and sat closer to the warmth.

The mind is an unwieldy creation. If short on answers, it will work nonstop to fill in the gaps whether wanting or not. The number of confused and contradictory thoughts rushing into his head at the same time was like drinking from a fire hose.

Murder? There is no doubt he rose from at least the first circle of hell, but a murderer? Did he really do it? Kill my mother? Of course he did. What's worse is I knew it. He almost killed me and would have if it wasn't for her pulling him off. And he would have finished the job if he had found me that night. Denial . . . denial . . . denial. Fool! All those lies. And I knew they were lies. He would never let her go. She never would have left me behind with him by myself. No . . . men like him never have a change of heart. They just change their story.

His brain did not give up without a fight, but every fight must end even if in a draw. He finally slipped into peaceful black silence. His reprieve lasted until sunlight poked through the curtainless windows. He woke to a room filling with the aroma of fresh percolating coffee. Jumbo was making a racket stoking the fire.

"Man, you were out of it," said Jumbo.

Carl stretched and looked outside to see the morning after. It was one of the prettiest sights Maine had to offer—a forest of frosted pines standing erect in military fashion on a blanket of white saluting a blue sunrise. That serene image popped like a soap bubble as a police car pulled into the driveway.

"We've got company," Carl said.

Jumbo looked out at the big bellied cop getting out. "Well, we knew they would come. Did you see who it is?"

"Yeah."

It was only a few seconds and a fist started banging on the door hard enough to shake dust off the rafters. Jumbo opened the door. Officer Charles Wickes brushed Jumbo aside and invited himself in. The officer stood six foot four and weighed at least three hundred pounds. His thick fur collared coat wasn't girdle enough to keep his mass from hanging over his belt. The ostentatious Wesson .44 Magnum on his side was probably more useful for stopping a buffalo stampede than stopping crime. He brandished intimidation like a weapon topping it off with mirrored sunglasses like a Mississippi chain gang guard. Carl and Jumbo knew him all too well.

"Where you been, boy?" he asked coldly.

"Right here," replied Carl.

"I've been looking all over for you," he lied. There was only one place Carl would be.

"Sorry," Carl said.

"Get your shoes and coat. Come with me."

Carl grabbed his stuff and walked up to the officer. When he saw Carl's face, he rolled his eyes and muttered some oath under his breath ending with "that stupid s.o.b."

"Get in the car," he ordered. Carl looked back impotently at Jumbo. Jumbo fantasized a red laser dot on the back of the officer's head as he put Carl in the back seat like a felon and drove off.

The drive to the police station was as cold and silent inside the car as out. Carl didn't ask why he was being taken. Officer Wickes didn't offer. As they rolled into the station, the officer finally spoke.

"What happened to your eye?" he asked turning completely around.

"Door," Carl replied turning his head away.

"Good answer." He paused. "Look at me." In a rare moment, he removed his sunglasses and looked Carl directly into his eyes. "Remember, this is your father and my friend."

Maybe he imagined it. Maybe not. But Wickes's eyes seemed to take on a coal fire cast as if another entity, more evil than he, was speaking. The message was unequivocal.

"Yes, sir."

"Let's go."

He took him through the double doors and down a hallway until they came to a door with a sign over it reading

Interrogation Room. "You wait in here. Someone will be with you shortly."

Interrogation Room? thought Carl. *Isn't that for suspects? Am I a suspect? Suspected of what? I didn't kill anyone. Maybe they think I was an accomplice!*

Carl could see Wickes's malevolent face every time he blinked as if the image were branded onto his eyes like a sunspot. He nervously scanned the surroundings. It was just like every interrogation room he had seen on the cop shows. Cinder block. No more than ten feet by ten feet. Painted sickly yellow. Harsh fluorescent lights overhead. The one small table and two chairs were clearly designed for a close, in your face, tête-à-tête. There was the standard one-way mirror, a speaker and a video recorder in the corner. He fidgeted for thirty minutes as his mind went rampant imagining all the nefarious things they were going to do to him up to and including water boarding. Finally he heard two men speaking outside the door.

"Did you do what I asked?" he heard one ask.

"No," was the reply. Carl recognized Wickes's voice.

"Why not?"

"You're the detective. It's your case, not mine," came the reply. Carl heard the heavy steps stomp off and fade down the hall.

The door opened. In walked a man of average height and build with thick dark hair and blue eyes, probably in his late thirties. He was wearing a shirt and tie without the jacket. His sleeves were rolled up. A detective's shield was clipped to his belt. No gun. He wasn't what Carl expected. *What's different?* he wondered.

"Good morning, Carl," he said reaching out his hand with a smile. "I'm Detective Luke Small."

He doesn't have that big me, little you attitude like Wickes. Carl thought. *Must be the good cop.* Carl rose and shook his hand. "Morning, sir."

"I'm pleased to meet you, Carl. I've heard a lot of good things about you."

Good things? What good things? "Pleased to meet you sir." *Maybe.*

"Has anyone been around to offer you anything? Something to drink? Juice? Coffee? What can I get you?"

"No, sir," he replied. "Coffee if it is no bother."

"Not at all. That's what this department runs on. And donuts, of course."

Carl made no response.

"Sorry, bad joke. Milk? Sugar?"

"Black, sir."

He opened the door and beckoned for someone across the hallway. "Sarah. Would you mind having someone bring in two coffees, straight up? Maybe some pastries and maybe a couple breakfast sandwiches from across the street?"

"Of course," she said smiling at Carl.

Before closing the door, the detective caught something out of the corner of his eye. "Hey, don't you have a case to work on? There's nothing around here that concerns you. My case. Remember?" Charley Wickes walked by the door looking like a caged lion lusting to attack its trainer but forced to bide its time for the right moment.

Maybe he is a good cop, thought Carl. *Anyone who can take on Wickes. Maybe I do like this one.*

Detective Small sat down in front of Carl. "Carl, I can see you're nervous. First of all, let me say you are not in trouble." Some of the fear dripped from Carl's face. "There are two reasons I had you brought here and the first one unfortunately is to give you some bad news. The only way to give it is just come out and say it. I'm sorry to be the one to tell you. Your mother is dead. Her body was found a week ago by some hunters not far from your house." The detective waited for his reaction before saying anything more.

Carl's face lost all expression. He just stared straight through the detective as if he were invisible. He knew. He had always known. But knowing all along she was dead made it no less shocking when the actual words were spoken aloud. A year of suppressed grief began welling up to the surface. The iron boy did something he had not done for a very long time. He sobbed.

The detective put his hand gently on Carl's arm. "It's OK to cry, Carl. Real men do."

Sarah walked in with some coffee and donuts and set them on the table. She gave him a look that reflected his pain. She handed him some tissues and quietly left them alone.

Finally the detective spoke. "Carl, are you OK? Can I get you anything?"

"No, sir. I'm fine," he replied looking away in embarrassment. That invulnerable exterior, his only survival tool, had finally cracked. He took the Styrofoam cup and sipped some coffee as if nothing had changed.

"Carl, we are treating this as a homicide. Are you able to answer some questions? We can do it at another time if not. There is no rush."

"I'm fine." Carl wiped his tears and returned to his stoic face, ready to engage with the detective. "You arrested my father for murder?"

"Actually, no, Carl."

Carl looked at him like that was the bad joke. "I heard . . .,"

"The rumor mill. It's typical. He's is in jail, but for assaulting an officer and resisting arrest."

"Is he getting out?" Carl asked.

"Are you afraid of him?"

Carl took another drink of his coffee.

"He's in the jail at least until he sees a judge Monday morning. He'll have to post bail, but, yes, if he can post bail he will probably get out," said the detective. "Let me be totally honest with you, Carl. Your father is a person of interest in this murder investigation. Do you know what that means?"

"I think I do," he replied.

"It means we have reason to believe that he's a suspect having some involvement with the crime but we don't have enough evidence yet to make an outright arrest. Our purpose for going out to your home was to inform him of the death of his wife and see how he would react. He took it very well. Too well, I would say. When we asked him to come down to the station for an interview, he knocked one of my officers down and bolted for the back door. He was also . . . well . . . drunk. But first things first. What happened here?" he asked pointing to his eye.

"Door," he replied losing eye contact.

Detective Small patted Carl on the arm. Then he put some documents in front of him. "Carl, these are some medical records I pulled. Believe it or not, we detectives do detect. Looks like you have hit a few doors in your time. Your mother also."

Carl took another look at this man. It didn't take a Sherlock Holmes to know he was lying. They all knew. But, was he serious? Why was the boiler plate answer that allowed everyone else to get on home to a hot supper now being questioned? Did he really care? Who was this guy?

"Carl, we need to build some trust here. I'm not the bad guy. I'm not going to hurt you. But we know who does, don't we?"

Carl just kept staring at the detective's face. *Are you for real? Is this the famous good cop, bad cop routine? Officer Wickes with his horns and tail on one shoulder and you on the other?*

Why should I trust either? Yes, I know who does the hurting. And so far I haven't seen much difference between the good guys and the bad guys. Is this just to use me to win your case and then dump me off to deal with the aftermath if it goes south?

In the silence, a still small voice joined in the conversation. His mother's. She had been silent for so long. "There will come a time," she said, "when you have to make a leap of faith. Appearances may say no. God will say yes. He will let you know when."

But why should I trust God either? He's treated me like I had leprosy.

The detective sensed the conflict in the young boy. "Carl, you have no reason to work with me. I know that. But I also know the truth and I know why you keep it hidden. I understand it. But now is the time to bring it all to an end. It won't get any better if we don't act now. It will get worse. I hate to say something corny like there is a new sheriff in town, but there is. You won't be doing this on your own. It's going to be you and me all the way. My job is to protect you and I will. Not just before and during, but after." He held out his hand hoping to seal the bargain.

The detective must have blown the right horn. Carl's mighty bulwarks fell flat as the walls of Jericho. "OK," he said taking his hand.

"Now, tell me what really happened."

Carl took a breath and started. "I went home to get some things and do some laundry. I usually do it on Friday nights when I know he's out with his buddies on a drunk. With the cold weather forecast, I decided to do it Thursday. I hoped he would be gone or passed out, but he met me at the door. He was drunk and immediately started swearing at the sight of me. He had an empty Jim Beam bottle in his hand. I didn't duck quickly enough. He threw it from across the room. He was a pitcher in school. Had a pretty good arm, they say. Turns out it's not bad when he's drunk either."

"I'm sorry, Carl. You sound like you don't exactly stay at home very much."

"Home?" scoffed Carl. "That's not home. I stay most of the time at Jumbo's."

"Jumbo?"

"A friend. Keme Lightfoot and his brother, Ben. They live about a mile away in the woods."

"So, how long have you been staying with them?"

"About a year. Ever since my mother . . ." He couldn't finish the sentence.

"Got it. You were afraid to see your father?"

"Stepfather," he corrected. "He's mean and a meaner drunk. It takes nothing to light him off. I try to avoid him. If I can't, I try to tip toe around him. It didn't work this time."

"For starters, Carl, I'll need you to fill out a complaint. That way we'll be able to get a protective order so he won't be allowed to get near you."

Carl's eyes opened wide. "That won't stop him. He'll kill . . ."

"No, he won't, Carl. I gave you my commitment. It's you and me. Together."

"What if he posts bond?"

"We'll be keeping a very close eye on him. He won't dare come near after I get done with him."

"But what about me? Where am I going to go?"

"Don't worry about that either. We are going to take good care of you. Are we OK?"

Time to take that leap of faith? Carl started to backslide. His mother's voice made one more appearance, "God says yes."

"OK," said the boy.

"Great. Carl, I would like to record this conversation. You don't have to agree if you don't want to. It just helps if we go to court. OK?"

"Yes, sir."

Detective Small walked over to the corner and turned on the video recorder and identified the participants, location, time and date.

"This will be hard, Carl. It always is. According to the Coroner, your mother has been dead for about a year." He pulled some more documents in front of him. "About a year ago, specifically on October 29th around ten o'clock that evening, 9–1–1 received a call from your home. An officer responded and filed a report saying it was a simple domestic dispute. He calmed them down and that was the end of it. He also has down here there were only two occupants in the house at the time. Is that true? I listened to the call and it sounded like a young man calling. He barely got the address out when the call was dropped. Was that you? Were you there?"

"It was me. I was there. But not in the house when Officer Wickes arrived."

"Tell me what happened that night."

Carl's face animated like a movie screen replaying a flick book of suppressed images all the time wondering if it really happened. Then he started. "My mother met my stepdad in AA. I wouldn't call him a father, but he mostly left me alone. He had a job. It wasn't bad. It was when he fell off the wagon things changed. He would get angry over the slightest things. He would get drunk and beat my mother and me over nothing. We didn't know from one day to the next who was going to show up, Dr. Jekyll or Mr. Hyde. Eventually we no longer had to wonder. Mr. Hyde was the only one who showed. My mother tried to make it work. When she finally realized it never would, she had someone make arrangements with a battered woman's shelter to take us until we could safely get out of the state. We had our bags packed and the car gassed up. He was already drunk when he left, but just as we were about to walk out the door, he came back. Forgot his wallet. When he saw the bags and us with our coats on, it wasn't a mystery what we were going to do. He went berserk. He said he didn't care about the bastard, me, but he would burn in hell before he would let her leave. He shoved her to the floor. I got between them and pushed him away. That's when I called 9–1–1. He grabbed his bat off the wall and started hitting me. I think he knocked me out. Everything was kind of grey after that. I remember seeing my mother pulling him off and him knocking her to the floor bleeding. He was standing over her with that bat. She waved me away and yelled for me to run. I crawled out the back door to the tree line. I kept fading in and out. I heard her screaming and him yelling. I kept trying to go back, but it was too late. Everything went silent. Then Officer Wickes pulled up."

"What did the officer do?"

"I don't know. I heard him yelling at my stepdad at the top of his voice. I could hear him calling him stupid out in the woods. Then it got quiet again. I could hear them doing something inside. Then Officer Wickes came out with a flashlight calling for me."

"What did he say?"

"He called my name. Said everything was OK now and that I could come back in. It was safe."

"You didn't respond?"

"No. I was scared."

The detective nodded. "Then what did you do?"

"I laid there until he gave up. I have no idea how he missed me. He's supposed to be a big woodsman. I was only ten feet from him. And there was a blood trail leading to me. Anyway, as soon as I could move without being heard, I crawled through the woods to Jumbo's house."

"It's OK, Carl. You're doing well. Do you have any sense of how long you were in the woods? When did the officer come out looking for you?"

"No. Not really. I just know I lay there a long time before I could move."

"Thank you, Carl. I know that was hard. Let's take a break. I'll be right back."

Carl sighed. He couldn't believe the words that just came out of his mouth. It really did happen. His hands stopped shaking. He was empty. They say the truth sets you free. He wasn't so sure.

Detective Small returned with two sausage biscuits and some fresh coffee. "Hungry?"

Carl nodded and reached for one. The detective took a bite out of the other.

"What else?" asked Carl.

"Let's unpack some of it. The timeline is very important. According to the report, Officer Wickes was there an hour."

"I'm not sure exactly how long," Carl said. "But it had to be longer than that."

"So, maybe two hours?"

"Maybe."

"But he was still there when you left?"

"Yes."

"Did you see anyone else come out of the house?"

"No. There seemed to be a lot of motion inside is all."

"Your mother's car. Was it still in the driveway when you left?"

"Yes."

"You mentioned a bat. You said he took it off the wall. What was it doing on a wall?"

"It wasn't just any bat. It was his pride and joy. It was autographed by Ted Williams. He was a big Red Sox fan. It was mounted on the wall on some big oak plaque he had made."

"Where is that bat now?"

"Gone. I don't know where. I never saw it again after that night."

"OK. You talk about Officer Charles Wickes like maybe you knew him?"

"Yes. He and my stepdad were buddies. They were two of a kind. He was just as mean only twice as big."

"And you mentioned Jumbo? You made it to his house. What happened then?"

"He took me to the hospital."

"What time did you get to his doorstep?"

"I don't know. It took a long time crawling on my belly along a deer trail. That's all I know."

"OK. We'll talk to him." Detective Small pulled out another document. "I have the medical report from that night. This certainly corroborates your story. It says you had a concussion, a broken left arm, two cracked ribs, and various bruises. Sound about right?"

"Yes, sir."

"Carl, the doctor filed a report suspecting child abuse, but we have no record of it here at the station. Any idea why?"

"No, sir. All I can say is Officer Wickes showed up at the hospital the next day and talked to the doctor. I think they wanted to keep me another day, but he had them release me. He wanted to take me back home. My mother left, he said, and things would be OK. I had such a fit, he dropped me off at Jumbo's and I stayed there."

"I see. And after that you went home?"

"Eventually, I tried," Carl said hanging his head. "It didn't take long to know that couldn't work. I just stayed with Jumbo. I didn't know what to do. I was confused."

Detective Small touched his arm again. "I know, Carl. I know. That's normal in situations like this. Don't beat yourself up. We'll file a second complaint on this report and a third for neglecting a minor. That will seal the deal on our injunction and we'll check for any more evidence of abuse within the statute of limitations. I have one more question. Did you ever call the police to either tell them any of this or to report her as missing?"

"Yes. A week later I called the Maine State Police. They told me to hold and transferred me to the Woodspring police."

"What did they say?"

"Officer Wickes answered. I hung up."

He switched off the video recorder. "Unbelievable. Come with me. I want you to meet a special person."

Carl followed him down the hall to another room. A petite lady rose from behind her desk. She had a small upturned pointed nose with bright blue eyes and highlighted hair.

"Carl. This is Eva Blankenship. She's our social worker and she is going to go over the next steps. She will take very good care of you. I will be back to go over the plan. I need to work on a few things first."

Eva and the detective exchanged a momentary glance that seemed to hang in the air long after he was gone.

"Nice to meet you Carl," she said. Her voice had a vaguely familiar tone.

V

DAVID MCKINLEY had already acknowledged his limited acumen for mathematics. Yet he was ready to challenge the ditty that one is the loneliest number that you'll ever do. He couldn't write the proof, but it was starting to be clear how two, even three, could be lonelier than one. The second person in the room, the only one who made him whole, was slipping away before his eyes while the third person, if he were around, if he existed, the omnipresent God, made no effort to stop it. It was a zero sum situation.

Mary McKinley lay in the cardiac unit of Massachusetts General. She was thirty six years old. Hope clung to hope from the time David revived her with the AED to the arrival of the EMT's and finally the Medevac to Boston. But now it was like grasping at a vapor. Her body was tense, stiff as if knowing she no longer belonged there. But it was tethered to earth, forced to remain by life support.

The dimly lit ambience with its incessant chirps, the continuous whir of the pump, and chemical smells added to the surreal feeling David had as he held her cold hand. He was there but he wasn't. The woman he loved was there but she wasn't. The life they planned was suddenly cut short like a film snapping half way through the movie.

Mary was the only one who stood by him through it all. She was the one who put him through grad school, the one who lifted him up when his novel failed. He was never holy enough for his pious mother, too successful for his henpecked drunk of a father, and his greedy sister had let him down, even after all he had done for her. They were all the same, out for themselves. Mary was all he had left.

Like dark filling the night, the familiar bell jar of helplessness descended over him. His only regret was children. That was their only real fight. She couldn't have any. "I won't adopt someone else's kid," he told her as she begged. "I don't care whose it is." That left an indelible scar on his soul that would chafe forever.

David's thousand yard stare was broken as he looked up to see Dr. Maxey darken the doorway. His face bore the heavy burden of a story repeated too many times. He walked over and sat down beside David. Words were not spoken. David hung his head. The doctor placed his hand on David's arm.

"Here we are again, eh, Doc?" David said breaking the silence in a whisper.

The doctor nodded his head.

"The end?"

"It's looking that way, David. We've searched every database. We don't have a match available. Hers is a rare blood type. We can't revive her."

"Yeah, I know," David mumbled, "the blood type. And I happen to be one of the few matches." He looked over at the physician with pleading eyes.

"No, David. It's not possible."

Despite knowing the outcome, the confirmation was no less of a shock. His mortal mind tried to process what was happening but it was like an algorithm trapped in an endless loop. There was no way out and no solution. Denial turned to anger as he remembered the cruel joke of six months ago that would have made Satan himself blush. There was a match. There was joy. Then, just as quickly, there was sorrow. It went somewhere else at the last minute. He tried to contain an eruption of rage against an innocent man.

"Tell me doctor," he asked, looking him in the eye, "what really happened that last time? What happened to the match we had?"

The doctor was staring at several layers of grief. He shook his head. "Honestly, David, I don't know. We had directed it here. Apparently there was another person higher on some list we were unaware of. I don't have a good answer for you. I'm sorry."

"Well, maybe I can enlighten you," David replied, his voice quavering. "I don't have a name, but I have it on good account it went to some rich, connected, alcoholic fat cat in Palm Beach." He looked at the doctor as if somehow that made a difference.

"Again, David, I don't know. We don't make those decisions. We're surgeons. Our only mission is to help people."

David's face transformed from anger and defiance to pleading in an instant. Tears streamed down his cheeks. "But, doctor, it's not fair. Can't we wait a while longer? Isn't there a chance one will show up in the next day or two?"

The doctor patted him on the back. "David, I know it's not fair. I see it every day. I don't have an answer for that either. Sorry. There is always a chance. Donors show up the instant they are available. But we can't wait that long." The doctor looked down. "I can give you thirty minutes."

The doctor waited as David composed himself. "Look, David, I might be out of line, but I got to know Mary pretty well during the course of her treatment. I don't profess to know the reasons things happen the way they do, but I certainly sensed that she did. I don't ever remember anyone that was so at ease given her situation. She called it having the single eye. She said God was in all situations for good even when it appeared to be evil. She said you just needed to see. Where that faith came from, I don't know, but I would give anything to have just a smidgen of what she had. I suspect she is grieving more for you than for herself." He stood up. "I'll leave you alone."

If I hear that one more time . . . condescending remark, thought David. *Everybody has a sermon. Like somehow that will make it all better. They might as well howl at the moon.* He looked up at the clock to start marking his last thirty minutes. That was all that was real.

But even the most devout atheist will bend his knee in hypocrisy when all else fails. And that is what David did. He got on his knees and prayed the same prayer as Jesus at Gethsemane that for some reason was stuck in his head. "Father, if it be possible, let this cup pass from me." But he left off the most important part.

And then his cellphone rang.

David reached over for his phone and looked at the caller ID. Perry Richardson. *God. You have to be kidding me. Is he calling me to defend my sister's honor? Now? It's a little late, Perry.* He pressed decline.

David returned to his knees one more time and prayed the same prayer. He gazed at his wife. He felt as lifeless as she. He tried bargaining with God. *Take me God. I'll face my sentence in hell. Just let her go.* Then, as if finally recognizing he had nothing with which to bargain, that he had no control, that he was totally at the mercy of the God he had been cursing, he added, "yet not my will, but yours be done."

Two nurses came in so quietly David almost didn't notice them. He started to panic. It was really over. They started making preparations. He had no idea the Grim Reaper actually had an empathetic face, but they did. That made it no better. His heart sank into his bowels.

Just as they were about to disconnect the IV's there was the sound of yelling from far down the hall. It was a familiar voice.

The nurses froze and stared at one another. David's head turned to see Dr. Maxey run into the room puffing for air. His body went limp when he saw he had made it in time.

He laughed and patted David on the back. "We have a heart! We have a heart!" Dr. Maxey looked over at the nurses. "Let's make some different preparations, what do you say?" He looked at David and laughed again. "You say you don't believe in miracles, eh? We have work to do." He turned and rushed out of the room.

David looked upward as if waiting for lightning to strike. Could this be happening? A miracle? Another cruel joke? He slumped down in his chair with the energy of a rag doll.

David watched the nurses work as he felt an out of body experience. Was he finally getting a break? He couldn't believe it. He watched as they wheeled his wife out of the room, hope now blooming like a desert rose out of dry ground.

David had been up for twenty four hours, but not one eye would close until it was over hours later. Adrenaline was pumping gallons a minute. He picked up some magazines but couldn't concentrate. The TV was blaring out all the world's woes but they were of no matter. He wondered if he should call someone, but he had no one to call. He looked at the recent calls on his phone. Perry had left a message. He pressed play.

"David, this is Perry," he said. His voice was hollow. "It's about your sister. She's been in an accident. Call me back."

VI

THE YELLOW cinder block cubicle was not much of an upgrade from his jail cell. Staring back at him was the face of a wiry middle-aged man with a grizzled beard, bloodshot eyes and hardened lines that added at least ten years. On the other side of that mirror was anyone's guess. Like a fox with one foot caught in a bear trap, his eyes vainly searched for a means of escape. The cheap clock on the wall was the only sound. The throbbing of his head and the tapping of his fingers were synchronized with each tick. The monotony kept building to a crescendo until the door finally opened.

Detective Small entered the room. "Good morning, Mr. Cook."

Kevin Cook did not trade amenities. He just stared at his captor like the offended party waiting for an apology.

"You know why you're here?" he asked taking a chair opposite him.

"Yeah," he grunted. "What's the big deal? Nobody got hurt."

"Well, assaulting an officer is taken a little more seriously around here. It could be a felony or a gross misdemeanor. We'll leave that up to the judge. Regardless, I need to make sure you understand your rights."

"Shoot."

Detective Small leaned over and turned on the video recorder. "We'll be recording this interview."

"Yeah, yeah, yeah . . . for quality purposes, I'm sure."

"Something like that. You have the right to remain silent. Anything you say can and will be used in a court of law. You have the right to a lawyer. You have the right to have one present during questioning. If you cannot afford one, one will be appointed for you. Do you understand these rights?"

He rolled his eyes. "Yeah, yeah."

"Would you like a lawyer present during this interview?"

"What for?" he replied smugly. "Got nuthin to hide."

Love the smart ones, thought the detective.

"Could use a cigarette instead of a lawyer," he smirked.

The detective pointed to the *No Smoking* sign over his head.

"Figures," he grumbled.

"OK, Mr. Cook," he said wasting no time, "so, to start with, why did you run when we came to your house last night? Why did you resist my officer?"

"I was just drunk and confused," he replied. "I done nuthin wrong. You guys had no business be'n in my house. I gotta right to drink in my own house. Ain't no law against it. You were going to arrest me for nuthin."

"Of course you have the right to do whatever you want in your own house. We weren't there to arrest anyone."

"You wanted to take me downtown," he argued.

"Just for some questions. Don't you remember why we were there?"

"Course not. Like I said, I done nuthin wrong."

Drunker than I thought. "Remember? We came to tell you your wife was murdered. We found her body a week ago? You said something like that was too bad for her."

Kevin struggled to pull some memories out of the fog. "Oh, yeah. I remember." He looked no differently than if he had heard the neighbor's dog had died.

"No grieving, eh?"

"Why? Sorry, but she left me a year ago. Guess that's what she gets. She had it pretty good. Shouldn't have left."

"Well, maybe so. But now it's a homicide investigation."

"What's that gotta do with me?" Kevin looked at this unassuming detective with renewed suspicion. "Say, wait a minute. What's go'n on here? What's that got to do with a assault?"

"Well, I don't know. You tell me. We came to inform you of her death. When we asked you to come downtown for some questioning, you hit an officer and tried to run. Doesn't that kind of make you a person of interest?"

Kevin tried to process what he had heard. "What's a person of interest?"

"It means you are not ruled out as a suspect. I'll ask again if you are concerned. Do you want a lawyer present?"

Kevin wondered why the detective kept pushing a lawyer. He studied Detective Small's poker face. They say if you don't know who the patsy at the table is, it's probably you. Kevin was a lousy poker player. He decided to call his bluff. "No. Like I said. Got nuthin ta hide. Only guilty people need lawyers."

"Then let's continue. Say, around the twenty ninth of October last year, where were you?"

Kevin looked at him as if there was as much hope as remembering the elements in the periodic table. "You kid'n me. I don't remember what I ate yesterday."

I've got an idea, thought the detective. "OK. Then when was the last time you saw your wife?"

"Dunno. Guess about a year ago," he replied.

"OK, close enough. About the time frame I just mentioned. Tell me about that," Detective Small asked.

"Nuthin to tell," he said turning his head to the wall. "She just up and left."

Detective Small pulled out a police report. "Nothing? Are you sure? Why would the police have to be called?"

"So, we had a little domestic dispute. Happens to everybody."

"Well, not so much. What was the argument about?"

"Her leaving me. I was mad. Wouldn't you be?"

"Did you touch her?"

"Course not. Just a little push'n and shove'n like all married people do. Mostly yell'n at each other."

"Why did she want to leave?"

"Got me. You'd have to ask . . .," he started. "A little late to ask her. Dunno. Like I said, she had it pretty good if'n you ask me."

"Who called 9–1–1?"

"I don't know."

"You don't have any neighbors close, so it had to be someone in the house."

"Guess that bastard son of hers."

"That bastard son of hers? What's that supposed to mean?"

"Carl. I adopted him but he's not mine."

"I see. There's no mention of him in the report. Was he there?"

Kevin looked up out the corner of his eye as if feigning recollection of events. "Yeah. I guess. For a while. He was running all around the house scream'n like a lunatic."

"Why was he acting like that?"

"Guess cuz she was gonna leave him. Look. I got stuck with feeding and tak'n care of him."

"Quite a burden, I suppose."

"Damn straight," Kevin agreed nodding his head. "I busted my ass for the two of them and look how I was rewarded."

"Tell me, where are you busting your ass these days?"

"Uh, well . . . I'm between positions at the moment," mumbled the suspect.

"So where did Carl go? He wasn't there when Officer Wickes arrived according to the report."

"Beats me. Like I said. He was act'n crazy. Last I saw him he was run'n out the back. Fell down the porch steps face first he was mov'n so fast. Clumsy bastard."

"You weren't concerned?"

"Figured he was OK. He kept going."

"Where?"

"Dunno. Ask him. He spends a lot of time with that injun on Beaver Creek."

"Well, Mr. Cook, he wasn't OK. According to the medical report the next day, Carl suffered severe injuries including a concussion and broken bones. You weren't aware of that?"

"New ta me," he replied shrugging his shoulders again. "He's always hurting himself. Can't track it all."

"Apparently both he and your wife were pretty clumsy," said the detective pulling some medical reports out of his valise.

"You said it," replied Kevin.

"Let me ask you straight out, Mr. Cook. Did you kill your wife?"

"Course not," he replied as if his virtue had been offended. "I let her go."

"You let her go," repeated the detective. "Did she need you to let her go?"

"Course not. Free country," he answered indignantly.

"Are you aware of anyone else that might want to harm her?"

Kevin's eyes lit up as if celestial beings were whispering in his ear. "I'd check out all those self-righteous Christians at that church she loved so much. Woodspring Baptist Church. Makes sense. Happens all the time with them hypocrites. Probably had an affair or something going on."

"We'll do that." The detective stopped for a minute and stared at his patient like a surgeon deciding where to make the next incision. "Mr. Cook, let's cut to the chase. We have a different version of events that night."

"From who?" Kevin demanded. "Nobody else was there except Charley Wickes and he wrote that report you got there that zonerates me."

"You and Officer Wickes are buddies, right?"

"What's that gotta do with it? What did he say?" Kevin's face revealed a few new shades of fear.

Detective Small continued like he hadn't heard him. "Look, Mr. Cook, we know you killed her that night, didn't you?"

"Hell, no. Why would I do that?"

"You said she left. Where did she go?"

"Told ya, don't you remember?" he replied as his voice continued to get harder. "She just took her bag and drove off."

"I see. Well, how is it her body was found only a few hundred yards from your house?"

"Beats me. You're the detective. You tell me. Maybe she came back for something. I dunno. Maybe she had second thoughts about that bastard son of hers. I would've gladly given him back. No need to sneak in the back from Libby Creek."

"What do you mean sneak in the back from Libby Creek?" asked the detective striking pay dirt.

"Uh, uh," he stammered like a fox with two feet caught in a bear trap. "Just a thought. Lot of deer trails and logging roads out there, around us . . . here . . . there, I mean, ya know, up by the creek. How do you even know she was murdered? Anything coulda happened. Log coulda rolled on her out in the woods at night."

"Log?" asked the detective.

Kevin glared at the detective. "Lotsa things can happen at night in the woods if you don't know what you're doing," he said trying to extricate that last foot from the trap. "There's, wuddaya call 'em? Woodsmen, mountain men, hermits that live out there in the woods. Live off the land. Poaching deer. You get in their way and all bets are off. This wouldn't be the first time. You city cops have no idea."

"Let's take a break," the detective suggested. "Coffee?"

"Yeah. Black." Kevin replied. If he could have removed his anklets, he would have gladly kicked himself in the derrière.

The detective got up and leaned his head out the door. "Sarah, couple coffees, please. Black."

"OK," she acknowledged and then nodded toward the Observation Room door as if there was something unusual.

The detective's confused look quickly gave way to a knowing nod back. He gave her a thumb up.

Sarah came in with two black coffees and donuts and set them on the table. Kevin eyed the female authority figure as if the world order had been turned blasphemously upside down.

Neither spoke as they sipped their coffees. Kevin gobbled down two donuts.

"Jailhouse food not too good, huh," chuckled the detective.

Kevin cracked half a smile. "You said it," and grabbed a third as if there were a time limit.

The detective let Kevin enjoy his moment. Finally he pointed to Kevin's wrist. "That's an interesting tattoo there."

"State Baseball Champs 1990." he said.

"Yeah. Seems I've seen that tattoo before. Oh, yeah. Officer Wickes."

"Yep. We were on the same team."

"Guess you guys are baseball fans. Red Sox?"

"What else is there?"

"Tell me about the famous baseball bat. I understand that it does exist?"

"Yep. Signed by Ted Williams," he said proudly. But that pride crashed just as quickly face down in the dirt. "Well, it did exist," he said correcting himself. "It was stole. Probably that bastard son of mine sold it."

"Worth some money, huh?" stroked the detective.

"Well, yeah," he replied as if its worth were as well known as the Hope Diamond.

"Was it stolen before or after you last saw your wife?" probed the detective.

He thought for a second. "Pretty sure it was gone before," he replied. "I don't really know exactly."

"Pretty sure? That's OK, Mr. Cook. I'll check the police report."

"Police report?"

"Sure. If it was worth that much surely you reported it stolen."

"Well, uh, actually I didn't . . . wasn't worth all that trouble," Kevin mumbled.

"I thought you said it was. Guess I was mistaken."

Kevin looked up like he had all fours and a tail caught in the trap now.

"So let's sum up a few things and we will call it a day. You did say that Mrs. Cook left on her own volition, correct?"

"I don't know nothin about no volition. She just up and left," he replied.

"Why didn't she take Carl with her?"

"Probably excess baggage, which is what he is. Left him to burden me."

"You keep referring to him as that bastard son. You don't like him do you?"

"Not relevant," he answered glibly. "I do what I gotta do. He's taken care of."

"According to word on the street, actually you haven't been taking care of him. He's been more in the category of homeless. You realize that's neglect of a minor, don't you?"

Kevin's eyes burned with hatred. "He's been taken care of," he shot back. "I don't have to track his whereabouts every minute. He's a big boy."

"I see, Mr. Cook. I think we'll wrap it up for now."

"Well, when am I going to get outta here so I can go home?"

"That's up to the judge. You have this assault charge. Now we have child abuse . . ."

"What the hell you talking about?" he yelled. "What child abuse?"

"Well, Mr. Cook, for assault and battery of a child on last Thursday, also on October 29th, 2015, and child neglect for the last year. That's for starters."

"I never abused nor neglected nobody."

"Like I said, we have a different version of events." Detective Small stood up. "And as far as going home, your house is now a crime scene being turned upside down. Thanks to your actions, getting a warrant really made our job easy. Thank you. So even if you were free, that is not where you would be going. Also, we will need a DNA sample."

Kevin sat there dazed like a bloodied bar fighter wondering how he ended up on the floor.

If I could get my hands on that bat, thought the detective, *I'd have everything I need.*

As Detective Small made it out the door he caught a large figure with a big iron on his hip disappear around the corner. *I'll take care of you later.*

VII

IT IS written that if your eye is single, your whole body shall be full of light. But if evil, your whole body will be full of darkness. Carl was seeing double. He felt like he was driving in and out a series of tunnels with alternating periods of light and darkness.

"Just one second, Carl." Eva Blankenship smiled at him as she moved her mouse around.

Her reassuring smile bounced off Carl. The light of justice that had dawned earlier was bending its knee to doubtful thoughts roaming through his head like ravenous wild beasts. *What am I doing? Why would I trust these people any more than the others? They don't care. If he gets out of jail, he's going to kill me too. What about Officer Wickes? And they won't be able to do a thing about him. It's all rigged. How could I be so stupid? Where am I going to go now? I can never go home.*

"Carl . . . Carl."

Carl jerked up as if awakened from a bad dream.

"Sorry, honey. Just had to pull up some information. I see you just turned sixteen. Congratulations."

"Thanks," Carl replied dryly.

"Guess you're thinking about that driver's license," Eva said with a half-smile.

Carl showed no emotion.

"Sorry. Maybe that's what we wish was the priority, right?"

"So, what is the priority?" asked Carl scaring himself with his boldness. "When is my stepfather going to get out of jail? What's going to happen to me?"

"That is what we are going to work on, Carl. I know this is hard. To have your entire world turned upside down."

Upside down? What do you know? When was it right side up? This isn't far from what I call normal. Except now it will be coming to an end one way or the other. Carl felt like a drowning victim reconciled to his fate.

Eva put her hand on top of his. "Carl. It's going to be all right. We are not going to let you down. I know personally that Detective Small will be joined at the hip with you from the beginning to the end. Trust us."

Us? Carl tried to reach into her soul for a sign only to be disarmed by her almost lucent blue eyes. If she had any guile, she was better than most at hiding it. But still, why should he trust her? It was a rhetorical question. He had already stepped off the building. If there is no net at the bottom, it was too late. There were no other options and the word of his interrogation would not remain secret for long.

"Let's start with some safe accommodations."

Carl raised one eyebrow. *Safe?*

"Relatives?"

"My mother was an only child of a single mother. She's dead."

"Anyone on your stepfather's side?"

"No."

"Your natural father?"

"No. He divorced us. Want's nothing to do with me. I wouldn't know where he is."

"Do you have a church? Anyone there that could help?"

Carl shifted into something more thoughtful. The conundrum of Woodspring Baptist Church. That was a good question. His mother loved that church. She thought they had loved them back. It was where he thought he had learned to believe and trust in a loving God. Now he wasn't sure. If God did exist, He and His church had abandoned him. He was treated as much like a stepchild of the church as he was at home. Too much trouble, he supposed.

"I guess not, ma'am," he replied with an undertone of disappointment that could not be denied.

"I see. Friends?"

"Yes," Carl replied attentively. "I stay at Ben Lightfoot's house a lot. They will let me stay there."

"OK. We can check him out."

"What do you mean check him out? I just said I have stayed with them all the time."

"It's OK, Carl. I am not ruling anything out. Anything is better than foster care or the county home."

"Foster care? County home?"

"Carl, as a minor, Social Services has to make sure you are in a safe place."

"Social Services? Isn't it a little late to worry about safety?"

"Easy, honey. We'll make it work."

"Why can't I just go home? At least until my step dad gets out of jail?"

"For one, the house is now a crime scene. It's all taped off at least until Monday. Secondly, as a minor you can't be left on your own. Except for special circumstances."

"What special circumstances?"

"For one, you need to have money to live on or have a job. Do you have any money?

"No money, but I can get a job," Carl replied. "My best friend's father owns the lumber mill in town. I work there in the summers."

"OK. And secondly you need to be able handle the responsibilities of being on your own."

"I have plenty of experience in that area," Carl said looking her straight in the eye.

"I believe you, Carl. These are some things for us to consider. For the short term, I don't think it's safe for you to be alone. It looks like Mr. Lightfoot may be our best bet. Let me hand that off to one of the deputies to check out and you and I go get some lunch. Hungry?"

His stomach growled like one of Pavlov's dogs to the word hungry. He followed her down the hall past rooms of white faces wondering which one would be judging his proposed red guardian.

As Eva passed Officer Wood, she handed her a piece of paper. "Sarah, would you please run a background check on Mr. Benjamin Lightfoot?"

"Of course," she replied.

Carl lightened up at her choice. Officer Wickes stood glowering at the three of them from the corner of the bullpen. His optimism went splat like a raw egg hitting the floor. This creepy guy was everywhere.

§§§

They say once a Marine, always a Marine. Chief Peter Sullivan in no way disparaged that mantra. Now in his mid-sixties, he still looked the part. Though gray now, his hair was always clipped short, his desk was immaculate. Everything about him said command and control. A veteran of Vietnam, his main theater of combat now was the battle of the bulge which he had held at bay fairly well. The only other pressing concern was keeping all his kids in one room and now, toward the end of his career, that looked like that might unravel.

His new detective rapped lightly on his door glass with his knuckles. He motioned him in and pointed at a chair.

"So, what do you have, Luke?" he asked.

Detective Luke Small made himself comfortable and gathered his thoughts. "Let me start with Carl, Kevin Cook's stepson. His testimony is that he and his mother planned on leaving Kevin because of physical and mental abuse. Kevin caught them in the act of trying to leave. He was drunk and pushed her to the floor. Carl intervened and was shoved out of the way. He picked up the phone and called 9–1–1 which is when Kevin pulled out a baseball bat, apparently a collector's item, and started beating Carl with it. His mother pulled Kevin off long enough for Carl to make it out of the house. Badly injured, Carl hid in the tree line until the police arrived. The last thing he remembers is Kevin standing over his mother threatening her with the bat. He didn't actually see her being killed."

"Who was the officer on the scene?" asked the Chief.

"Officer Charles Wickes."

The Chief dropped his head. *Always something.* "Go on."

"Carl made it to a friend's house, a Jumbo?" the detective said looking at his notes. "He transported him to the hospital where he was admitted. Concussion, broken arm, cracked ribs. The doctor on duty filled out a suspected abuse report which was picked up the next morning by one of our officers."

"Wickes?"

"Yes, sir. It never made it into our system. Anyway, we will go back and retroactively file child abuse charges on that as well as the most recent event which happened Thursday night."

The Chief looked at him in disbelief, his head involuntarily wagging like a bobble head.

"As far as Kevin Cook's interrogation, he was read his rights and declined the offer to be represented by legal counsel. He of course denied anything to do with her death stating she wanted to leave and he let her. It makes no sense, though, that Carl was left behind. The only thing he has going for his story is the fact that she did quit her job and clear out her bank account just before her disappearance. Her last day at work was the night in question. She apparently did have plans to leave and according to Carl, it was to make it to a battered woman's shelter. We are trying to track down which one that might be, but we know the answer to that. She never made it. We have other medical records indicating numerous injuries for both Susan and Carl. They all have the markings of physical abuse but there never were any formal complaints. That would have helped us. He made several incriminating remarks, including knowing where the body was and suggesting the manner of disposal, but right now it is all circumstantial."

The Chief nodded again. "Did you find any evidence in the house?"

"No. Supposedly the violence went down in the kitchen. We used Luminol, but if there were blood splatter, it had to have been cleaned up by someone who knew what they were doing."

I wonder who in town has that skill? thought the Chief

"We have enough to charge him, but I am sure our DA is going to say we need something more tangible to seal the case. We really need the bat which we are sure was the murder weapon. The cause of death was blunt force trauma. By someone with significant anger issues."

"Yeah," said the chief. "Unless we are dealing with the keystone killers, that bat is long gone."

"One would think, but this guy is really quirky. I think if we give him enough rope, he'll do our job for us. They always do. There are a lot of things we have to run down. Also, I hope you agree, we need to recuse Officer Wickes from any part in this investigation."

"This is your case, Luke. That's what you were hired for. You handle it however you deem fit. The last homicide we had around here was about thirty years ago. A teenager collecting paper money went missing. Found him the following Spring in the same general area as this one. The body was stuffed under a log just like this one."

"Did they find the killer?"

"The chief at the time turned the investigation over to the State Police. They didn't spend much time on it. Said it was probably an accident. Maybe the log rolled on top of him, they said. Closed it out."

"Guess the kid wasn't related to any of the Kennedy's."

"You got it."

"Thank you, Chief. I'll be interviewing Officer Wickes this afternoon. One other thing. Carl has requested that we place him under the guardianship of a Benjamin Lightfoot that lives out on Beaver Creek, apparently in some little cabin. The only concern showing up is a bar scuffle a couple years ago. I figure you know all the characters in town."

"I do," agreed the Chief. "Ben is a Marine. Iraq war veteran. Bronze Star recipient. Enough said?"

"Yes, sir," agreed the detective. "Sounds like the kind of man I'd like to have my back."

The chief nodded. "I remember that incident. Ben is a hard drinking Indian, but he is also a hardworking man who keeps to himself. A couple of skinheads stepped in it mouthing off against the war. When they decided to spice it up with a few ethnic remarks, that was all it took to get them banded to a stretcher. I killed the officer's charges."

"Who was the responding officer that night?" asked the detective.

The chief cocked his head at his detective as if to say "you don't know?"

The chief watched his new detective walk out the door. *Charley Wickes, what legacy are you going to leave me? I can't protect you anymore, son of my best friend or not.*

VIII

OFFICER CHARLES Wickes may have appeared to be calm as he took his turn in the interrogation room, but inside he was more like a cobra quietly coiled up in a wicker basket ready to strike as soon as the music stopped. That might be a while. Hatred surged though his body. He didn't know who or what to curse first. If he could scream, he was certain it would break the soundproof glass separating him from the observation room.

Kevin, he thought, *what an idiot! Has he never heard the proverb that a man who has himself as a lawyer has a fool for a client? That's why they're proverbs, fool. They are always true. You never talk to the police without a lawyer when you're a suspect! And absolutely not when you are a person of interest in a murder investigation. Look at the position you put me in!*

Then there was Detective Luke Small. He could hardly get his name and the word detective out of his mouth at the same time. The city boy. The college boy. *The guy who took the job I should have had. Me, with twenty two years on the force and passed over by someone from away? And now I have to sit here and answer to that smug little know–it–all with his big words. He may think he's that smart. We'll see about that.*

Knowing he might be watched, he checked himself in the mirror. He smoothed out his contorted face and pulled a comb out of his back pocket and slid it several times through his thick black hair. He couldn't help but admire the touch of gray at his temples.

He went over Kevin's testimony in his head and rehearsed what he would say. He was as ready for the detective as he could be. The bat was the one thing that kept burning in his gut like indigestion that no medicine could cure. *I hope that idiot burned it like I told him. I even lit the fire for him. He was more sorrowful about having to part with that bat than his wife. Unbelievable. I should have stayed and taken care of the last few details. It's always the details that make or break a case. If he had another bottle stashed . . . well . . . who knows. I should have checked for that too. Too late now. I won't have a chance to talk to him till he makes bail. Our stories have to be consistent.* He wagged his head, a thing that seemed to be contagious around the department that day.

Finally the door opened. "Good afternoon, Officer. Sorry to keep you waiting."

"That's OK, Detective. I know this case is keeping you busy."

"For sure," Detective Small agreed. "I know you're busy too, so we'll get right to it and get you out of here. Since this is a murder case, and you may have been one of the last to see the victim alive, I hope you don't mind if we video your interrogation?"

"Be my guest," answered the officer forcing the muscles in his mouth into a smile. *Never let them see you sweat,* he kept reminding himself.

Detective Small went through the formalities of having him state his name, rank, etc. for the record. "Officer Wickes, let's start with the police report you made out as the responding officer to a 9–1–1 call on October 29, 2015. Looks like you showed up on the scene around twenty two hundred."

"Yes. I arrived. I found a typical domestic dispute. I'm sure you have as much experience with them as I do."

"I do. So what were the circumstances of this domestic, as you say, dispute?"

As I say. What's that supposed to mean? He thought stilling his anger. *Don't let them see you sweat.* "Apparently she wanted to leave him. He was upset about it. Understandably."

"Understandably. Of course," repeated the detective.

Why does he keep repeating me?

"So, go ahead and just run through all the events. It looks like you left around twenty three hundred, about an hour later?"

"Yes. When I arrived, they were doing the typical yelling, screaming, pushing, and shoving. The first thing I did was separate them and find out what the issue was. Once I ascertained what they were fighting about and learned that she was determined to leave, I held Mr. Cook back until she loaded her vehicle and drove out of the driveway. He had no right to keep her. That's about it."

"So you saw her drive away?"

"That's what I just said."

"What about the boy, Carl? I don't see any mention of him in the report."

"He wasn't there when I arrived."

"So all that took an hour?"

What's he up to? They looked like two sumo wrestlers slowly surveying each other's face for an advantage. "I stuck around a bit to calm him down."

"OK, so you were there for an hour and that was it?" asked the detective.

What does he know? wondered the officer. "I might have stayed longer."

"But the report says you left at twenty three hundred."

"It does. Because that was the end of my shift. I was off the clock. I stuck around a while. Like I said, he was upset."

"I see. You and Kevin Cook are buddies?"

"I don't know if I would use the word buddies. He and I go back to high school. It's a small town."

"But you share a lot of interests? Both Red Sox fans. Kind of hang around together watching games, maybe drinking? I'm not judging by the way."

"Some."

"So, how would you describe Kevin Cook? You probably know him as well as anyone."

"Just a regular guy. Liked baseball. Was good at it in his time. Probably drinks too much, but that's not a crime if you're not behind the wheel."

"You never knew of him to be abusive to his wife or son?"

"No. Had no reason to."

"Officer Wickes, there have been two other 9–1–1 calls in the last three years. Each time there seems to be a trip to the emergency room for one or both. Each time you seem to be the responding officer. And each time there was no abuse charges or formal complaints, yet it seems to be as obvious as an arsonist leaving a burning house with a can of gasoline and a lighter that that is exactly what was going on."

Like a bull being suckered to a red flag, Officer Wickes had an intense urge to gore his opponent. *Don't sweat.* "What are you insinuating? Are you trying to tell me I don't know how to do my job? It sounds like I'm more a suspect than he is. This is going to be the end of this interview. Just who do you think you are?" The officer stood up.

Detective Small made no effort to stop him. "You can end it whenever you want to," he said shuffling his notes nonchalantly.

You . . . I'll fix you later. The officer kicked himself for being played. He sat back down.

"All I'm saying, Officer, is that there were classic signs any novice police officer should have been trained to detect . . ."

That knife hit its mark with ninja precision. "If you have a problem with my detective work, you can take it up with the chief," said the officer through his teeth.

Then he twisted the knife. "I'm just saying that sometimes there can be a blind spot when you are dealing with people you are close to."

"I never said we were close."

"Let's be blunt. According to lore, Mr. Cook was just a plain old drunk and a mean one at that. Apparently common knowledge, yet you're saying you never saw him exhibit those traits?"

"No. I never did."

"OK, let's move on. Let's talk about the famous bat Mr. Cook allegedly owned. Signed by Ted Williams, worth substantial money. Are you aware of its existence?"

"Yes."

"Do you know where it might be?"

"No. It hung on the wall. He had it mounted."

"Well, it's not anymore. Bat or mounting. Just some holes in the wall. But you say you don't know where it is? If it were stolen, sold, whatever, destroyed?"

"I do not."

"Never noticed it was gone?"

"Sure, I noticed it. But I never asked what he did with it."

"Interesting. Something that both of you would have valued and no one said a thing."

The officer's cheeks turned a darker shade of red.

"So, you have been to the house a few times since you noticed it was gone?"

"Not that much." The officer replied.

"OK, let's move on again. Carl. Apparently unbeknownst to you, he was there that evening. He was the one who called 9–1–1 and ended up in the hospital. The following morning you show up at the hospital and had him released. Were you called there to investigate something?"

"No. I just had an early shift and was making some rounds. I happened to find out he was there because the doctor flagged me and said he had a boy with a few injuries. And it wasn't unbeknownst to me that he had been there earlier. Kevin told me that he had run out of the house when they started arguing. He was upset and tripped on the way out."

"A few injuries? Concussion. Broken arm. Cracked ribs . . . Some trip."

"Again, Detective, what are you insinuating? I'm not a doctor. What are you implying?"

"I'm not insinuating anything. I know you're not a doctor. That is why we rely on them if they suspect child abuse. He says he reported it to an officer. I assume that was you. What happened with that?"

"I don't recall. If I got it, I put it in the system. Sometimes they get lost. But, like I said, I already knew what happened."

"Then what did you do?"

"I explained to him that his mother had left and I would gladly take him home. He didn't want to go home. He was still very upset. I took him to that Indian's cabin on Beaver Creek. That was it. Are we done?" asked the officer. "We seem to be going around in circles. I've told you everything I know."

"Yeah, were done. For now."

You're right. For now, thought the officer.

Detective Small got up and moved toward the door. "One last thing, Officer," he said in parting. "We need a DNA sample from you so we can eliminate your DNA from any evidence we find in the house. Also, you are recused from any part of this investigation given your relationship with the suspect. You will have no contact with Mr. Cook or any of the individuals involved with the case. Clear?"

The detective turned and stepped out without waiting for an answer. Officer Wickes stayed seated as the door closed behind the detective. The music stopped. His eyes turned into slits and he made a guttural sound that sounded more like a hiss. *I've got two loose ends to take care of*, he thought to himself, *you may have made it three.*

Chief Sullivan stepped out of the observation room. He looked over at the detective, wagged his head one more time, returned to his office and closed the door.

IX

COUNTRY ROADS may take people home, but that doesn't mean they all like it. That last curve was as eye opening as any rumble strip as David's passenger side tires started sliding on the gravel shoulder. "Easy," he muttered. He, of all people, knew that those yellow speed limit signs should be viewed as more than a mere suggestion. *The only good thing about this trip*, he thought, *is this will be my last time.*

A lot competed for attention with the road. Mary's heart transplant was successful and her convalescence was going well. But now he had to leave her alone in Boston to attend his sister's funeral. His feelings ran the gamut from elation to guilt over their last conversation to inconvenience. *Why would she want to buried back here in the woods?* He just shook his head.

What an unbelievable reversal of fortune, he thought. *Two heart stopping events with diametrical outcomes. We finally get a break and my sister, who had it all, gets killed on a South Florida highway.* Mary never called her new heart a miracle. That surprised David. She made it sound like it was a natural and normal thing, like God did this stuff behind the scenes all the time. David called it serendipity. Mary called Deborah's death one of God's mysterious plans and that somehow, good would come of it though we may never know exactly what. David called it fate and there was nothing good about it.

David hit a patch of black ice. The unwanted thrill finally convinced him to take a little heat out of his drive. *What's the rush? She'll still be dead regardless of when I get there. I don't need to join her.* The mid-morning sun was still hidden on the other side of the leafless hills leading him on to his birthplace and a childhood he would prefer to have left behind. He hated each and every mile. Ice and trash trimmed the river edges below. *Same as ever. Nothing changes.*

He was getting close. Fessberger's farm, if you could call it a farm, was coming into view. *That guy was crazy. Trying to raise pigs and goats on the side of a hill. But I have to admit, he did it. These hillbillies know how to make something out of nothing.* That at least drew a modest chuckle, something that had been in short supply for some time. Some things were worth remembering. Like the day one of Old Man Fessberger's goats hung itself on the front lawn. Or the day he and Billy Redstone got caught messing with his pigs only to come face to face with a disheveled old guy in long underwear with a shotgun. That was funny. However, he was a better shot than they estimated. Picking rock salt out of Billy's rump wasn't pretty. *You can't make this stuff up.*

Things got a bit more sober as he rounded the next curve. There it was. The landmark. To any passerby, it seemed benign enough. It wasn't much to look at; just a white clapboard building about the size of a one room schoolhouse set on a hill with a simple steeple and cross. It was the words over the threshold that used to torment him as if being poked by the devil's personal red hot pitchfork: ***HOLINESS OR HELL,*** in big, bold letters.

He slowed down almost to a stop to stare down his demon one last time. *Too bad,* he thought. *Had to be one or the other, didn't it? No middle ground? No compromise? Nothing in there for me. Not even purgatory? How about a holy hell? If there were such a thing, this would be it.* He thought he had conquered those old feelings, but those words never seemed to lose their affect. It was too late. He had touched a match to dry kindling.

His name was Frederick William Sunday, aka Billy Sunday, his namesake. He would march up and down the aisles during his sermons getting up close and personal with his sheep. "Hey sinner man . . . sinner woman . . . do you know Jeeesusss? Are you right with the Lord? Or do you want to burn in hell. Repent and receive Jeeesusss," he would squeal in falsetto as he twirled around the sanctuary so as not to miss eye contact with anyone.

Hell was no respecter of age. "What about you, son? You go'n to heaven or hell? Thems yer two choices. That's where yer head'n if you don't receive Jeeesusss. Repentance or hell. Holiness or hell. What'll it be?"

He was baptized to the delight of his pious mother with the hope nightmares of demonic grotesques shoveling hellfire over his head would cease. They did not. But it did send Pastor Billy Sunday in search of other sinners to save. The pastor may have failed to scare the hell out of the ten year old boy, but pretty much succeeded in scaring the holiness out of him.

The little white house came up on the left, a two bedroom cracker box he had called home for eighteen years. "Home sweet home. The great inheritance," he murmured. *It wasn't the money*, he thought to himself as he traded Pastor Sunday's wrongs for his sister's. *It wasn't worth much. She can have it all, like she needed it. In the end, what good did it do her? It was the principle. I was criticized just because I made my way out of this backwoods hole and never looked back. I was not appreciative enough, they said. I turned my back on my mother, they said. I wouldn't help when she fell ill. What could I do about it? I had a career to build. I had to pick myself up by my own bootstraps. I was ashamed, they said, because she was uneducated, an embarrassment. It was easy for Debbie and that pretentious husband of hers. She had everything handed to her on a silver platter. I had to work for everything.*

And Perry Richardson. What a beaut. Mr. Perfect. Ivy League. Old money. Who the hell does he think he is? Calls me up at a time when my wife's life is hanging by a thread. Was he insinuating I was to blame? Says her cell showed her on the phone with me at the time of the accident. Wanted to know what her last words were. What gall! Anybody driving in South Florida does so at their own risk.

David burrowed ahead like a horse with blinders until he was right on top of his turnoff. It was too late. He floored the brakes leaving an ugly set of black stripes in the rear view. He screeched the car into reverse and swerved onto the short access road. The iconic red brick funeral home with its roman portico columns came into view. *Best looking house in the county and it's for the dead.* The same shiny black limousine that carried his mother a year ago was parked in front ready to go, a solemn plume of vapor trailing straight up in the still air.

He could see Perry and Jess and Bess, all three with matching black wool overcoats, standing out front greeting mourners. The lot was full. David checked his watch. Just in time. He had to drive around back to find a spot. He wondered how many would show up for his funeral. *I'll save myself the embarrassment. Scatter my ashes to the four winds. . .just not here.*

He stepped out of the car and buttoned his coat as the cold slapped both cheeks. "Let's get this over with," he said to himself.

The unconditional love of children has a way of heaping coals of fire on the enemy's head. He was no sooner around the front when the eight year old twins spotted him. "Uncle David," they yelled and threw their arms around him. He couldn't help feel the poison being sucked out of his soul. He leaned down and returned the affection, wondering what it would have been like to have had his own children. He thought of Mary and her love for children. Maybe it wasn't too late. They had a new start. It was the first time he felt human in a long time. He was ready to meet and greet.

Perry Richardson waited for him on the porch before walking in. He always did the right thing. David had no reason to dislike Perry, but there was something that made him uneasy. He was honest enough to admit it wasn't Perry that created the disconnect. For someone who had it all, movie star good looks, wealth, status and personality, he was just as at home with Maine country bumpkins as the Palm Beach crowd. His lack of guile disarmed everyone but David. *No one's that good,* he thought.

Perry spoke first. "Good to see you, David," he said with his hand held out. "Sorry it has to be this way."

David nodded. "Yes. Good to see you too, Perry."

"Is Mary doing OK?" asked Perry.

OK? Doesn't he know what she just went through? Thoughtless. "She's fine," is all he said.

"Good."

They walked into the sanctuary with no more to say to one another. It was full except for the reserved row in the front. The forms of dress ranged from ill-fitting three piece suits to overalls. David looked over at Perry pleased he had left his Armani suit at home. He always knew what to do. They shook a few hands. David nodded to some other familiar faces embedded in the pews.

The casket was closed. The damage from the accident was more than the skilled hands of the mortician could undo. Pictures of his sister were surrounded by so many beautiful flower arrangements it was like navigating through a garden. Hidden between two baskets he found a picture of Deborah's graduation at Orono. She was excitedly kissing David on the cheek waving her diploma wildly in the air. He remembered how proud she was. How proud he was. He felt a new guilt rising up tasting rancid like bile.

As the participants gathered on stage, David froze. There he was—Billy Sunday. *Still alive. Must be eighty,* he thought. His pompadour hair was just as thick as ever, only snowy white. Their gazes locked for an instant. His stomach tightened up just like when he was a child. But the old "evil eye," as he called it, seemed to have lost some of its bite.

The choir began with *Just As I Am,* Deborah's favorite song. Jess and Bess sat between David and Perry. They looked so sad. David unexpectedly found himself wiping a tear for them if not for himself. Perry was staring into space with a peaceful look as if he were somewhere else, maybe on a desert island or a mountain top alone with Deborah saying their goodbyes.

Billy Sunday stepped up to the podium. David braced for the hell-fire the pastor so wanted sinners to feel well in advance of the judgment. He started with a verse from 1 Corinthians 13:

"For now we see through a glass, darkly; but then face to face: now I know in part; but then shall I know even as also I am known"

"We all has the same question," he said. "Why'd a good God, a God who sez he's love, allow such a beautiful person, a beautiful Christian, to be taken fore her time. It don't make sense to us. It can't make sense without faith. I could say that all things work together fer good to those that love God, but without faith, we cain't understand. Faith sez God is ever where, all the time, in ever circumstance in our lives. But without the Holy Ghost, we'll never see Him. We may see a tragedy. God sees something different.

"Why'd Deborah leave us so soon? I dunno. I do know that I'll know some day. That plan may not be showed up until the end but it will be showed up. An in that plan, God's love will be showed to'a been at work. We walk by faith, not by sight . . ."

Is this the Billy Sunday of old? wondered David. The man who couldn't wait to get his hands on hell's burners to make sure it was hot enough? The temperature in that room never rose above a comfortable warmth. *Even articulate in his own way,* thought the man of words. *What changed? Him or me?*

Perry walked up on stage. His usually controlled manner gave way to raw emotion as he gave a loving eulogy of his wife, best friend, lover and mother. Tears wet the benches as one friend after another came up to the podium with words that displayed a love and admiration usually reserved for saints. When the last chance came for any others to speak, shame glued David to his seat. He wanted to say something. But he couldn't. Maybe he owed someone an apology. Maybe he owed a few.

The choir sang one last song, *I'll Fly Away,* as the pall bearers came and picked up the casket. The procession was trailed by Perry with Jess and Bess and then David. The line of cars gave new measurement to the proverbial country mile clogging the two lane road to the cemetery as traffic patiently waited for them to pass. Pastor Sunday delivered a few last words of comfort. Again David wondered who this guy was. Then it was over.

As David started to get into the limo to go back to the funeral home, he saw Perry talking to a lady in her mid-thirties. *Is that who I think it is?* he wondered. *It is. They stayed in touch all these years.* He thought about going up and talking to her. *No. She wouldn't want to talk to me.* He got in the car. He had much to think about on his ride back to Boston.

X

IT IS written that the wages of sin is death. Detective Small had seen many cash their final paychecks on the streets of Boston, but this case didn't fit that axiom. Susan Cook was a quiet, reserved, intelligent, church going woman. Not much was known about her past. She had no social media presence. By all accounts, she seldom talked about herself but was always an ear to those in need. Her maiden name was Russell, originally from Skowhegan. That changed when she married Lawrence King, presumably Carl's biological father. That marriage only lasted a short time. Then she married Kevin Cook. *Maybe on the rebound?* wondered the detective.

She worked as a bookkeeper for Morris Lumber Products. She never missed a day, always on time, always flexible to work any hours. One Friday she collected her last check and politely blindsided Mr. Morris with notice she would not be back. And she wasn't. It was clear she did not want anyone to have advance knowledge of her escape plan.

The yellow lights in the old office seemed to be fading in and out. He wasn't sure if it was the poor wiring or his tired eyes. He was clear, though, that they had their man. The question was did they have enough circumstantial evidence to convict? He kept replaying the same old newsreel over and over in his head searching for anything they missed. *What was his motive? She was the breadwinner. Was that what enraged him? No more golden eggs from the goose? We have no blood evidence in the house. Obviously a professional cleanup. We don't have the missing vehicle. We know they lied about seeing her drive away. We don't have the murder weapon. Her quitting her job with clear intent to leave doesn't help our case. No . . . We need some hard evidence.*

Bail had been set at $30,000 for assault and child abuse. The detective knew Kevin Cook didn't have the money to make bail and, for some reason, he wouldn't or couldn't put the house up for collateral. *I'll have to check that out. One thing for sure, there is likely to be at least one hero to come to the rescue.*

He listened to the 9–1–1 tape one more time. "9–1–1. Please describe the nature of your emerg . . ."

"Help . . . help," screamed a boy's voice. "My stepfather . . . he's gone crazy . . ."

"Calm down," the voice said. "Give me your name and address and tell me exactly what happened."

"Carl Cook. Avery Road, RR1, Box 256. My stepdad, he's crazy drunk . . . I think he's going . . . to kill . . ."

There was a dull thud and the line went dead. The 9–1–1 operator called back. The line was busy. She dispatched Officer Wickes who, according to her, had an understanding with the dispatcher to be assigned to any calls dealing with Kevin Cook's residence. *Interesting.*

The detective listened a few more times. He could barely hear some groans in the background. *Not intelligible enough for evidence.*

He read Officer Wickes's skimpy report one more time. The Incident Type said "Domestic Disturbance." The narrative was one short paragraph: Arrived at Kevin and Susan Cook's house at 10:04 p.m. responding to 9–1–1 call. Residents were upset. Some yelling and pushing. Calmed residents down. Neither willing to file any complaints. Left scene at 10:59 p.m."

What a ridiculous report and what little is there is a lie. Just have to prove it. No mention in the report he watched her leave like he said. Or what the dispute was about. Said he left around eleven. Carl is sure Wickes and his mother's car were there for much more than an hour. The timeline is weak, though. And that bat. Where is it? It has a name. It's called Blunt Force Trauma.

The banging on his door kept getting louder until it finally broke his spell. He looked up to see her peeking at him through the blinds in his door. He waved her in.

"Hi, Sarah. Sorry. Working late aren't you?"

"There's a lot going on," she said. "I have some information about the case."

"What do you have?"

"Cook made bail," she said,

"That was expected," he said. "Anybody we know?"

"Anonymous," she said with an eye roll.

"Right. Let's get patrols setup around Beaver Creek. Do we know where he will be staying?"

"Not yet. The house is still cordoned off with police tape. We are waiting to see what he does."

"OK, keep an eye on him. He did have his passport revoked, right? Canada isn't very far."

"Right."

"Anything else?"

"Yes. A couple interesting things. Looks like Susan had a life insurance policy." Sarah placed a document in front of him. "Carl is the beneficiary."

"That's good news. Substantial sum. I'll get with Eva. She can work with Carl. That gives him more options."

"One last thing," she said putting a manila envelope in front of him. "All the DNA analyses we asked for."

The detective pulled the papers out and studied them. He looked up at Sarah. "Now that wasn't expected. Let's keep that to ourselves for the time being. I don't know if it's relevant to the case or not. Good work, Sarah."

"Thank you, sir. Good night."

"Good night."

§§§

The elephant in the room meme took on new meaning for Carl as he passed through the cafeteria line. The news had exploded about his parents. The *Bangor Daily News* and the *Portland Press Herald* ran some back page stories but for *Woodspring Weekly Word*, it was the story of the century. Despite the lack of detail in the nascent investigation, it unabashedly plastered the headline in the biggest, boldest fonts that would fit across the front page:

Murder Comes To Woodspring, Maine
Husband a Person of Interest

Carl felt like he must be living in some ethereal dimension unseen by earthlings. People's lips were moving but sounds were muffled. Eyes looked straight through him like he was transparent. He took his chicken sandwich and fries and sat down across from Andy Morris, the lone inhabitant at the end of the table.

Andy, Carl's best friend, was the only one lately who wasn't treating him like he had the plague. His father owned Morris Lumber Products where Carl's mother had worked as a bookkeeper. Despite being the rich kid in town, Andy failed to make the in-crowd scene for various reasons. They were branded "rich boy, poor boy."

Andy compared his amply laden tray to Carl's. "Is that it? No packed lunch today?"

"This is it. Had enough Spam."

Andy laughed. "I'll bet Jumbo has a hearty pantry." He wasn't kidding.

"I need to get to the store and help him out. We could stand to expand on the two food groups we have."

"Can't be too bad."

"I'm not complaining. Bacon and eggs every morning. I need to get my own place, though. I've mooched off him a long time."

Andy's chubby cheeks turned a warm pink at the thought of sizzling bacon before taking the hint. "Oh, Yeah, well, I talked to Dad," Andy said. "No problem. He needs the labor on Saturdays. Nobody works on Sunday, of course. Minimum wage."

Carl nodded. "Thanks. It's a start. Somehow I have to get some more money. They said I had to be self-sufficient in order to be out on my own recognizance."

"Sounds like you're the one trying to make bail."

"Really. It feels like I'm locked up in the Twilight Zone." Carl looked around the room. "Say, is it my imagination, or is it awfully quiet around here?"

"Around you, I'm afraid. Everyone's buzzing."

"So, I'm not paranoid after all. Maybe they think I'm a killer too. Like father, like son you know. You can tell them we aren't blood. Not to worry."

"That's not it," assured Andy. "I think it's more . . . well, I mean, your face kind of tells it all. They don't know how to react."

"Yeah. Killer look I suppose."

Andy dug into his lunch with an appetite commensurate with his anatomical requirements. Carl picked at a few fries as they ate in silence. Suddenly Andy, with mouth open full of food, froze as if an avenging angel had descended from heaven and turned him into a pillar of salt.

Carl put his sandwich down. "What is it?" He was afraid to turn around.

"Anyone sitting here?" came a pleasant voice.

Carl looked over his shoulder. It was an angel all right complete with golden blond hair down to her shoulders. The new girl stood behind him with a tray. Carl knew her from a distance albeit that distance was only two seats in his AP journalism class.

He had wished he had the nerve to talk to her, but she had two qualities that stopped the boy from the other side of the tracks. She was pretty and she was smart.

"Fo . . . no," said Andy, the only person Carl knew who could fumble a word like no, as he swallowed that last bite whole.

With her hands full, Carl stood up and pulled out a chair. "Please," he said. *She must not know of my infamy*, he thought.

"Thank you," she said sitting down. "Sorry. Looks like this is the only place left." Then she blushed. "Sorry . . . didn't mean it like that."

Carl looked at the several vacant chairs separating them from the next group of diners. "No offense taken. As long as you're not," Carl replied.

"My name is Kathy", she said holding her hand out to the two of them.

"Nice to meet you, Kathy. I'm Carl and this Andy. His father owns the sawmill in town." He didn't know why he said that.

"Yes," Andy chirped in proudly, "nice to meet you."

"Nice to meet you. I've only been here a month. I'm from away, I guess, as you call it. Boston."

"Ayup," joked Carl clumsily only to join the other red faces. "That's what we call it." For a second, he forgot who he was. Then he saw the jocks staring at him. Suddenly he had taken on solid form. "You know, maybe we should leave. You may not know who . . ."

"I know who you are," she said. "Please stay." She removed the plastic from her salad, smiled, and started eating.

Carl looked over at the moonstruck face of Andy as if to agree. *Maybe there is a God after all.*

"You guys going to the basketball game tonight?" she asked.

"No," answered Andy. "Sports and I don't exactly see eye to eye."

"Oh, that's too bad. I'm excited. I just made the cheerleading squad. I was lucky since I started the term late. How about you, Carl?"

"I think I'll make some games, but this week . . . well, it would be difficult with my schedule."

"Understand. Say, I wonder when Mr. McKinley will be back. That was a crazy writing exercise last week, wasn't it? Really got the creative juices flowing."

"Yeah, for sure," agreed Carl as his mind took an unintentional U turn back to that emotional tsunami that almost drowned him. *Why did I write all that stuff? He must think I'm a psychopath.*

"You all right, Carl?" asked Kathy.

"Yeah . . . yeah." Her sparkling blue eyes snuffed out his dark thoughts. "I was just thinking how right you were. He really got us thinking."

"What did you think, Andy?" asked Kathy.

But Andy didn't hear. For a second time in ten minutes he turned to a pillar of salt. By the look on his face, this one had to be the real avenging angel.

Carl and Kathy turned to look.

"Detective Small!" exclaimed Carl.

"Hi, Daddy," said Kathy.

Carl looked at Kathy wondering if this was a pity thing or an ambush.

§§§

Eva Blankenship stood in the school conference room as Detective Small escorted Carl through the door. Carl wasn't surprised. Nothing surprised him anymore.

"I'm so glad to see you again, Carl." She reached out and shook his hand. "Please sit down."

"Carl, I'm sorry for pulling you out of school, but there are some developments happening fast that we need to share," said Luke.

Fast? That's one way to describe it, thought Carl as he tried to read both of them at the same time. *Is this good or bad? Guess I better buckle up.*

As if reading his mind, Luke answered. "It's one of those good news–bad news things, Carl. Any preference?"

"Bad news," Carl replied prepping himself with his stoic mien. *Let's get it over with.*

"Your stepdad made bail this morning. As we discussed, it was more a matter of time."

"Officer Wickes?" said Carl as a statement more than a question.

"Presumably," replied the detective. "Anyway, we're not ready to charge him with murder . . . yet. So, for now the charges are assault on an officer and child abuse."

"How did he take that last one?" asked Carl knowingly.

"Not too well. That is why we need to take some measures. We are going to increase the patrols out by Beaver Creek. Do you have a cell phone?"

"No."

"You do now," he said handing him one. "My and Eva's numbers are programmed. That's the bad news, but we do have some good news."

Good news? That won't take much. The bar isn't very high.

"Eva? Do you want to cover some of his options?"

"Yes, Carl. Your mother had a life insurance policy, fifty thousand dollars. And you are the sole beneficiary. Now that we have a death certificate, you can collect that immediately."

Carl's eyes flickered for a second but the cost of this good news quickly snuffed out the flame. He hung his head. "You mentioned options," he said finally.

"Yes. Remember we talked about you being on your own. You would need to be financially and mentally fit to make your own decisions. It's what we call emancipation of a minor and by all accounts, you qualify. We should have no problem finding a judge to rule in your favor. If that is what you want."

Carl's mind sifted through all this rapid fire information. "So, you're saying I can be on my own? Like an adult?"

"Yes, Carl," interjected Detective Small, "but let's be wise about this. Given the 'bad news' we just discussed, we feel safety should be the number one consideration. Staying with Mr. Lightfoot is still an option. I know he is perfectly capable of defending himself, but he's not there all the time and the location isn't ideal for police protection. We'll have patrols cruising through there, but there will be gaps in time. Staying in town, would be much safer."

"Where would I stay in town?" asked Carl.

"You can stay with me and Kathy," said Luke. "That would be the safest."

Carl looked at him and then Eva. Eva was smiling as if she were part of the plan. "Why would you do that?" he asked.

"Like I said, Carl. I'm with you all the way. And so is Eva. It's not an inconvenience at all. We have extra rooms. I take Kathy to school every morning. Two birds with one stone," he joked.

Carl just stared at the detective. *Does he really mean that? He seems to. All of a sudden everyone cares?*

They waited as Carl processed these new options.

"You don't have to decide right now," said Eva. "You can think it over."

"What if I want to go home?"

Detective Small sighed. "It's an option, but I strongly recommend against it. You would be alone and the location would be just as difficult to ensure your safety."

"Where would my stepdad go if I did that?"

"He wouldn't like it, but he would have to go some other place. He won't be able to get near you with the protective order."

The room went silent again. He thought about the beautiful Kathy. He thought about his independence. *I've done OK without anyone's help so far*, he thought.

"That's his problem."

XI

BEING THIRTY five thousand feet closer to heaven didn't provide any more clarity as Perry Richardson fingered the little red book in his lap. Jess and Bess were across the aisle, sweetly passed out on each other. Their young minds knew in part, but time would not spare them from the full understanding and pain of what they had lost. The flight attendant came around to refresh his wine glass. Perry held up his palm. She nodded. They seemed to know those that were riding the long black train.

The mind has a protection mechanism. It spins a cocoon around itself to ward off extreme pain, but it doesn't last. At the time, it feels warm and moist inside, but it inexorably sheds, leaving the soul naked to the bitter cold realities of life, death, and grief. A tear trickled down his cheek. *I was wondering where you were*, he thought. He no longer fought them. He pulled out his handkerchief and returned his attention to the red diary.

So this is what haunted you for so long, Deborah McKinley Richardson, he thought as he turned the pages to September, 2000, Freshman year–UMO. *What you wanted so badly to tell me but couldn't.* He leaned back in his seat remembering her joking, "You can read it when I'm dead. Then you'll know all my dark secrets." She would laugh, but the laughter thinly veiled the sadness. She let the book lay in an unlocked drawer for years as if hoping he would find out for himself what she couldn't bring herself to confess.

To Deborah McKinley, Yale Law School was about as likely as a backwoods Maine girl marrying a Palm Beach jet setter. Yet both happened. She never considered applying to Yale. Someone told her about their need based programs. "Why not?" she said. "Who would have thought," she said, "that being below the poverty line would make Yale the least expensive option?" She met Perry Richardson in her contracts class. He was rich, she was poor. He was sophisticated, she not so much. He came from a prestigious prep school, she from a state university.

He smiled as he remembered how awkward she seemed navigating her first year classes with alumni and faculty whose names alone evoked fear and reverence at the same time. He would sit behind her and watch as she chewed gum and nervously twisted her hair while taking copious notes. When it came time to team up on a project, he could see her start to panic. He slipped her a note asking her to be his partner. She turned around and looked at him for the first time. He fooled her, she later told him. He had that "look" of the rich, but it was different than the phonies that masqueraded around campus. He made her feel safe.

Perry felt a tingle inside every time he remembered the "look" she had. He loved it and never told her for fear of scaring it away. Beyond the overdone makeup and the bright red lipstick, she was a refreshing sea breeze in contrast to the pretentious tropical winds of Palm Beach. She had jet black hair, huge dark brown eyes, high cheekbones accentuated by an aquiline nose and weighed all of a hundred pounds. She was beautiful.

He delighted watching her expressions as he showed her another side of life that had lost most of its shimmer for the rich.

"You call that a boat?" she said staring at his father's yacht.

He shrugged his shoulders with a mischievous smile.

"When you said it was parked in your back yard, I assumed it was like Uncle Jim's outboard sitting on a trailer with weeds growing around it. Your backyard is the Atlantic Ocean."

"I didn't lie, did I?" he teased.

"Well, ain't you something," she replied.

But it would take more than Yale Law School and Palm Beach to quell her demons. He was so comfortable with who he was, no matter where he was, always full of confidence. She seemed to be in a constant state of tension. The opulence, the wine, the song, everything about this new world had her mother droning in her ear, "sin." And then there was the other thing.

She was amazed to find the rich kid that grew up with the silver spoon was just as much a man of faith.

"Jesus said his yoke was easy and burden light. Why are you weighed down so?" he asked her.

She just looked at him.

"He didn't come to accuse us, honey," he told her. "That's just unbelief. We have an accuser. You need to stop listening to him. Jesus came to save us from sin, to forgive us, to set the captives free. What are these chains you keep clanking behind you like Bob Marley?"

"I have secrets," she told him.

"We all do," he laughed.

"I mean *real* secrets," she said checking his eyes for seriousness.

"OK, hon," he said sensing a struggle. "When you're ready, I'm ready. Either way, it doesn't change a thing between us. It doesn't change a thing between you and Jesus. He has already forgiven whatever it is."

"Maybe," she said. "But that still leaves me."

That time never seemed to come. But now he knew.

He caught himself starting to drift to sleep from the sound of the great jet engines. He was still on the same page. He called it *The Book of Deborah*. He started through the parts he had highlighted one more time.

September 1, 2000
Here early, Somerset Hall, Room 216. I think I am going to vomit. My roommate is Lizzie Mills from Skowhegan. I know nothing about her. I pray she will like me.

September 2,
Lizzie is sweet. She is going to help me with my makeup. Actually I don't have any. She says I will never make it here with no makeup and my hair up in a bun. She asked what hills I came out of. She's funny.

September 15,
Sorority Rush. Lizzie says I have to pledge. Otherwise I'll be left out. She says Pi Beta Phi.

September 29,
Hurray, I think. Lizzie and I are in. Had my first beer. I'll be going to hell (if Mother finds out).

October 21,
Bob!!! I think I'm in love. From Sigma Chi. He is so tall and skinny, like a beanpole. He towers over me. Black curly hair with bushy eyebrows and Abraham Lincoln cheekbones. A Senior. He is going to be a mechanical engineer.

November 14,
Bob invited me to his house in Rockland for Thanksgiving. Can't wait to meet his family.

November 28,

The Castello's are so nice. They have a fleet of lobster boats, which Bob means more than one. He says it's not the life for him. He says he's not going to war for turf, or surf, whatever you call it, with all those redneck pirates.

March 1. 2001
OMG. Lizzie bought me the test. This can't be! What will I do? I'm a whore. Going to hell for sure. What if Mother finds out?

March 3, 2001
Bob says get an abortion. It would be best, he said. We're too young to have a child. It would destroy our lives. He has job offers. I think he's going to leave me.

March 21,
Told David, the only one I can trust. He says abortion too. Says my life is ruined if I have it and forget about ever going home. They'll try an exorcism on me, he says. He may be right.

April 14,
Met with Planned Parenthood. Options are limited. They seem friendly enough, but there is something creepy about that place. Maybe it's their eyes. They're hollow, like predators figuring out how to divide the spoil. Appointment set for April 21. Protestors out front. Handed me a bill. "Free Sonogram." Bob has an offer from a company in California.

April 21,
Skipped classes. Skipped Planned Parenthood. Did the sonogram instead. A heartbeat, but something irregular about it I think. The technician gave me a funny smile but said nothing. Maybe to calm me down. Is something wrong and they won't tell me? Help me, God. I can't do an abortion. That is murder. They won't be chopping up my child. David says I'm a fool.

May 15,
Haven't heard from Bob in a month. Won't return my calls. I know he took the job offer in Los Angeles with Northrup Grumman. Guess he picked a place as far away from Maine as he could. Guess David is right, I am a fool but only because I loved.

June 2,
Still conflicted. What do I do, God? David still says abortion. Liz says adopt. They almost fought about it. Getting late. I don't know. Where are you, God? Is this the only way? Planning one more trip home. Just a slight baby bump. I don't think Mother will notice. I'll blame it on the ice cream shop on campus. I've done everything else. I might as well start lying. Lizzie's mother says I can spend the summer with them in Skowhegan. I told Mother I had a summer job there. I'll see her when it's all over.

The flight attendant placed a hot cup of coffee on his tray. Perry flipped through the pages until he got to November 1.

OMG. Labor twenty four hours. Declined the epidural. I deserve the pain. I just don't believe this. How could this be? Could God make it any harder? Where are you, God? What do I do now?

November 2
Gone. Social worker wasted no time. I'm in shock. No tears. It's beyond that. What have I done? More than my flesh is gone. My heart is torn out. I hate myself. I hope I burn in hell with Judas. We are both betrayers. I deserve worse.

Unbelievable. Perry's tears made an encore appearance. His gut twisted and turned as if he were the one giving birth and losing his child. That was the last entry in Deborah's diary. She never wrote a single word after that. Or so he thought.

He flipped the empty pages to the end. *What's this?* There was one last entry on the last page he hadn't noticed. It had no date.

Perry, if you are reading this, then now you know. Please forgive me. I want you to know that I did finally learn to forgive myself. It wasn't easy. Your faith and that of your family are what healed me, though I know you don't realize it. I went from seeing a God of wrath, of hellfire and brimstone, to One who IS Love, patient, kind, forgiving. I know now that there is nothing our God cannot forgive. Praise Him!

I love you. I love Jess and Bess. I love all my children, some of whom you do not know. I pray for all of you. Whatever the circumstances are that you are reading this, I trust God has done all things according to His will for a purpose. Know that I will be with you always.

I Love You Forever, Debbie

Perry closed the book and leaned his head back just trying to absorb it all. He felt like his heart had been ripped out. *Why did you take this burden on all by yourself?* he thought. *I was there for you. That was my job. But I am so happy that at last you found peace in yourself.*

His mind went back to funeral and what he had learned from Deborah's college roommate, Lizzie Mills.

"I thought you knew," she said.

"No. I knew there was something that haunted her for years. She wanted to tell me. But she bore it alone like a martyr. It must have been awful."

"It was. I know we never talked about it after that day. It was painful to watch her every time she would run into a young mother. I thought her heart was going to jump out of her chest."

"Was it a boy or a girl?" he asked.

"I guess you really don't know. She had one of each." Liz braced for the shock.

Perry looked like she could poke him over with a finger.

"Do you want to sit down?" she asked.

"She had two sets of twins?" he said almost in whisper as he took her advice.

"Yes. That was what was what was so amazing and why her pain was so great. More than double. That's why she never could talk about it."

"Do you know where they are?" he asked as if in a daze.

"I know who adopted the boy. It was a friend of mine from Skowhegan but I have no idea where she is. She got remarried and dropped off the grid."

"What about the girl?"

"I have no idea. That was totally unexpected. Those free clinics never told her she was carrying two babies. They took her away the same day, but I don't think even Deborah knew who adopted her."

Who are you that I don't know, Jess and Bess's sister and brother? Perry let the jet engines do their job. He put his seat back and passed out.

XII

AND THE sign said:

VICTORY BAPTIST CHURCH
The church with the money back guarantee

That's a new one, thought Detective Small as he rolled into the parking lot. *I thought it was Woodspring Baptist Church. Wonder why they changed the name?*

The detective made his way toward the back of the church where the offices were. A young lady in her twenties greeted him.

"Good morning," she said exhibiting two rows of ultra-white teeth. "I guess you are Detective Small."

"I am," he replied distracted by more cleavage than he expected in a Baptist church. "Good morning."

"Let me show you to the pastor's study. He's running a little late counseling some newlyweds."

"That's no problem. I'll just make myself comfortable." *Maybe look around.*

"May I get you some coffee?"

"Thank you but no. I just had some before I left the office."

"He'll be with shortly." She smiled and turned toward the door.

The detective watched the shapely girl leave. *Pretty girl.* Then he started his usual perusal of the surroundings. Centered above the credenza was an engraved wooden sign with the quote, *God Helps Those Who Help Themselves.*

I'm no theologian, thought Detective Small, *but I'm pretty sure that is not in the Bible.*

He walked around the room taking stock of everything, all of which seemed to be relatively new. The desk, the bookcase, and the credenza were all matching solid cherry with ornate moldings. *Pretty rich for a little country church.*

He went around the desk to peruse the books in his library. What people read was equivalent to the proverbial picture worth a thousand words. There were several books of sermons, various commentaries including a complete set of Matthew Henry Commentaries, Bibles of different translations and several, he assumed, Christian best sellers. There were pictures and awards filling the voids.

Except for a laptop, the desk was completely clear of any papers or books. An elaborate gold pen holder stood at attention above a blotter that appeared to have never blotted anything. The visitor chairs were symmetrically canted toward his desk chair. He looked down at the floor. The carpet looked like it had been laid that morning. Everything was tastefully coordinated in light grays and dark blues. The cleanliness would put any reputable hospital to shame. There was not a speck of dust anywhere. *OCD?*

The screen saver circulated a school of crosses swarming like an overstocked goldfish bowl. Two elaborately framed certificates on the wall caught his attention. One was a Doctor of Divinity degree from Esoteric Theological Seminary awarded to Glen M. Huff. *That's a new one,* he mused. Another one displayed a certificate in Spiritual Counseling from another unheard of school. He withdrew one of the commentaries from the bookcase. The spine cracked slightly as if it had never been opened before.

"Good morning. I am Dr. Huff," came a deep resonant voice behind him.

Startled, Luke jerked around. "Good morning, Pastor . . . Doctor. I was just admiring your library." He stuffed the book back in its hole and walked around with his hand out. "I'm Detective Small."

The pastor was younger than he had imagined, maybe late twenties. He was about Luke's height with slender hands and perfectly manicured nails. His hair was so coal black he wondered if it was dyed. The dark suit accentuated his fit build while his green eyes had a curious look like that of a cat examining a canary.

"A pleasure, Detective. A bit of a theologian yourself?"

"No . . . no. Still working on the Good Book."

"Well, that's a start. Please sit down and tell me how I can help you this morning."

As Luke sat down, it felt like he would never hit the bottom of the plush seat. He found himself looking up at his interviewee, an awkward reversal for someone usually in control.

"As I said on the phone, I am investigating the Cook murder. I am trying to find out as much about the family as I can . . . their marital relationship, family members, their relationship with church members. It's my understanding they were members of this church?"

"Ahhh . . . yes, of course. They were members. Unfortunately, I never got to know them that well. I have only been here less than two years."

"Of course. We'll just work with what you know. We can start with some basics. Were they regular attendees?"

"As I recall, she was pretty regular. I don't remember Mr. Cook so much."

"What about their marital relationship. Were they having any problems? Did he, she, or they ever come to you for help? Perhaps for some counseling?"

"Well, she did come to me once for spiritual assistance. It was shortly after being called here as Pastor."

"I see. Is spiritual counseling different somehow than plain old marriage counseling?"

"It is in the sense that the problem is irrelevant. We treat the root cause. All problems stem from some form of spiritual illness as their source."

"Hmmm . . . I guess you mean sin?"

"Exactly," he replied.

"Well, was their specific form of spiritual illness, or sin, manifesting itself in marital problems? As police, we kind of need to be more specific."

The young pastor paused to choose his words. "Well, the fact that she requested counseling suggests they were having issues. No disrespect, but as a detective, you know I am limited in what I can reveal about our sessions. That is held private under the same umbrella as a confidential doctor–patient or lawyer–client relationship."

"Well, just tell me what you feel comfortable with without sacrificing your oath." *We'll worry about a subpoena later.*

"Of course. I think it's public knowledge their marriage was in trouble. She wanted to leave him, to divorce him. I told her that divorce was a sin and shared what the Bible had to say about wives submitting to their husbands."

"How did she take that?"

"She listened. We shared other scriptures. We prayed for the marriage. That was about it."

"I see. And what exactly were the issues they needed to have resolved? Or, as you might put it, what were some of the symptoms of their spiritual issues?"

"Like I said, Detective, the perceived issues are really irrelevant. They all have the same resolution in Scripture."

"I understood that," replied the detective acknowledging his condescension. "However, the transgression of worldly law isn't quite so generic. It's based on specific transgressions. Sorry to press you, Doctor, but the symptoms are what laws are based on. Was there any evidence of or claims of abuse? Physical or mental?"

The pastor's eyes narrowed as he reassessed his persistent visitor. "No, Detective. I don't recall that there were."

"Within that year period that Mrs. Cook did attend, there were some trips to the ER with facial lacerations and bruises. If she attended regularly, surely that was noticed by you or others in the church?"

He had a thoughtful look for a second. "No. Sorry."

"What about Carl?"

"Who?"

The detective paused. "Carl. Her son. If she attended regularly, he would have been with her."

"Oh . . . yes. I remember."

"He also was not unknown to battery. No one noticed?"

"Sorry."

"Let me ask you, Doctor, were you aware she had stopped attending church?"

"Of course. I heard that she left town."

"And Carl. He remained in town. Did he continue to attend?"

"Now that you mention it, I don't think so."

"No one checked on him? Being fifteen at the time, no one considered he would need transportation to make it to church?"

"Unfortunately, the church isn't large enough to support a bus ministry and I suppose we would have assumed his father would bring him," the pastor said.

"I guess you didn't know his father. I'm sure there are plenty of people in this church who did. Too bad someone couldn't swing by and pick him up. He's an awful nice kid. Let me ask, were they a significant source of revenue for the church?"

"I wouldn't know the giving record of anyone in this church, Detective," his deep voice taking a defensive tone. "Everyone is treated the same."

I hope not, thought the detective.

"I will check into some transportation for Carl. I must admit, that is egregious," the pastor said. "No excuse, but we have been very busy. Apparently our deacons haven't been able to keep up with all the new members. The congregation has doubled in the last two years and it is unfortunate that someone might have slipped through the cracks."

"Oh, how many new members do you have?"

"About two hundred," he said.

"Maybe you'll have that bus before you know it. So, who is the deacon for the Cooks?"

The pastor pulled a notebook out of his lap drawer. "Let's see. Looks like it is Howard Bates. He teaches at Woodspring High School."

The detective climbed out of his chair and straightened his back. "I'll be sure to talk to him. I think I have all I need for now, Pastor. I guess I'll find you here if I have any more questions?"

"Not for long actually, only a couple more weeks. I have been called to a church in Kentucky."

"A larger one I assume."

"A little bit," he replied. The pride shining through the thin veneer was blinding.

"Congratulations. Looks like you, at least, are doing well."

"God helps those who help themselves," he replied with a grin. "Oh, you might want to contact my retired predecessor, Pastor Joe Theriault. He knew the Cooks much longer than I."

That wouldn't take much, he thought as he responded, "I have him on the list. Thank you for your time." They shook hands.

The detective passed back through the small sanctuary. *I wonder where all these new members sit,* he wondered. *Anyone looking for God might want to keep looking. I think He's left this building.* He walked out past the administrative assistant. *Pretty girl, though.*

XIII

IT IS written to count it all joy when you meet trials of various kinds. Those were the last words Howard Bates tried to utter before they were stuffed down his throat by David McKinley. David looked over at his wife in the passenger seat. He was finally looking at joy. But it didn't make sense that he had to go through such flames to get there.

His joy was now permanent, but the feelings associated with it were more of an ephemeral thing. Doubts and cares take little bites out of it like incessant termites until there is nothing left but a hollow shell.

Mary finally broke the silence. "What's the matter? You've been awfully quiet this whole drive."

"Nothing," he muttered as he turned off I–95 onto the two lane that would take them home to Woodspring.

"I know you better than that. Something is eating at you. Look at your face." She reached over and changed the angle of the rear view mirror. "You should be happy. What is it?"

David's convicted face looked into the glass. "I don't know. It just seems like things have happened so fast that somehow we . . . well, it seems like we got the bum's rush and now we're left flapping in the wind again."

"What do you mean? Dr. Maxey said a typical hospital stay for a heart transplant is seven to fourteen days. We stayed ten. And my surgery was so successful and the match so perfect, it couldn't have gone any better. We should be thankful."

"I am. It's just that I thought there should have been some home care while you were convalescing. I called our insurance and they said it wasn't covered."

"So? If we needed it, I am sure Dr. Maxey would have said. I feel fine."

"It's not just that," he confessed. "I argued with them and asked why the six months of daily nursing care we had before the surgery was covered."

"And?"

"And they said it wasn't covered. They didn't know what I was talking about."

"Oh . . . so what are you worried about?"

"What if we get a bill for that? Can you imagine how much that would be? We'd be out on the street."

Mary looked straight ahead and sighed. David's face turned a paler shade of white. Mary was not one provoked easily, but it was possible and David just made it so. And when that line was crossed, the alleged blockhead would be schooled in the error of their ways. David was that blockhead. And he knew it.

"I'm sorry. I didn't mean it that way," he said placing his hand on hers. But it was too late.

"You know, David. I love you. I love you more than anyone else in this world ever will . . ."

"I know," he mumbled.

". . . It wasn't me I was concerned about through this trial. It was you. I was going to be fine either way."

David looked over at his wife speaking sternly to the windshield as if maybe it would listen. He knew she meant every word. Her faith had always been a bright beacon but somehow his self-imposed thick spiritual cataracts managed to block most of its light.

"And I know how you hate to have me preach or quote scripture, but some things are self-evident that you just don't get."

David hunkered down keeping his eyes fixed on the road as he prepared for the imminent come to Jesus moment.

"I understand that somehow you were damaged in your Christian upbringing. You need to get over it. I also know that whether it was painful or not, you walked away with plenty of Bible knowledge. Remember the parable of the sower?"

He nodded not making eye contact like a child sitting in a corner with a pointy hat afraid to speak or turn around.

"Good. Well, you're the seed that fell among the thorns. You are so consumed with the cares of this world and how much you don't have that you can't enjoy what you do have. How much time have you spent fuming about how much your sister had and how unfair it was? And had is the word. She no longer has anything. Does that make you feel better? As I remember your sister, she loved you dearly, was generous to all around her despite what you say to the contrary. She in no way affected us or harmed us or had malice toward us. God had a different plan for her, but that could just as well have been me. God clearly has another plan, not for just me, but for us. We don't know what the total plan is, but this I can tell you, it should be an adventure, not something to fear. So what if we go bankrupt? Us being together is not enough? Remember that shoebox apartment we started out with? I don't remember it being all that bad. I was teaching first grade. You were writing your novel. We were always broke. Those were some of our best times." She turned to her husband. "Tell me, Do you believe in miracles?"

David's face went from pale to pink. He dared not deny or affirm.

"Well, you should," she said turning sideways and staring him in the face. "You just witnessed one. A bona fide miracle. That's an argument you won't win. If you think that last minute reprieve was luck, you would be very wrong. And as far as the nursing care goes, I didn't order it. Apparently you didn't. Maybe you're looking at another miracle. Accept it. Did it ever occur to you that God is right there in every single situation and just might know what He is doing? Let Him do His job. Take a load off."

The car went silent as a tomb except for Mary's slightly elevated breathing.

Suddenly David started laughing and couldn't stop. She looked over at the unexpected reaction.

Finally he said, "That felt so good. I just realized how much I missed my mother's tongue lashings. That was so cleansing. Thanks, Mom. I needed that."

Mary shook her head and laughed. "Now that's better."

"I love you," he said.

"I love you too." She reached over and held his warm hand. "At least we tested out the new heart. Looks like it should be good for a few miles."

"We sure did."

Mary's sermon may have moved the needle, but that didn't stop the termites from chomping. *How does this plan work? My sister's death. How is that part of the plan? That's a tall glass of water to drink. If He has a plan for me, He's running out of time.*

§§§

David tossed out the crunchy papers scattered in his driveway except for the *Portland Sunday Telegram* and the *Woodspring Weekly Word* which he set neatly on the coffee table to thaw. Mary was taking a nap. It would take months for her body to completely recover from her ordeal. David poured himself a cup of coffee and settled in his easy chair wondering what cuisine delight he could conjure up for dinner. It was a limited menu. He took the Portland paper first to start reading but the unusually bold headlines of the *Weekly Word* underneath grabbed his eye—**Murder Comes To Woodspring, Maine**. He set the Portland paper aside and slowly picked up the *Word* with no less shock than if it had said Martians had invaded Woodspring.

Susan Cook. Body found by hunters. Classified a homicide by the coroner. Detective Lucas Small handling the investigation. Kevin Cook is a person of interest. He couldn't believe it. *I remember her*, he thought. *Carl's mother. She came to that first parent—teachers conference when he was a freshman. She was so petite and meek, but full of determination. Someone not to be taken lightly when it came to her son. Carl was definitely her biggest priority. She had so many questions about the journalism class. Carl wanted to become a writer, she said, and she wanted to setup a private conference to discuss writing as a career. What schools should he consider? What books should he read? What types of writing genres should he consider? She was so well spoken. I told her as long as he didn't mind being a starving novelist, I would be glad to sit down with them. That didn't matter, she said. This is what Carl wanted. I wondered why she never came back. What a shame.*

Immediately he thought of Carl's disturbing story; penned so eloquently yet so, so dark. *It makes sense. He was crying out for help. But it was too late. There was no one to help him. Were there other signs?* A tingling shot up his spine just like when one wakes up in the middle of the night knowing the answer and not liking the taste. *Of course there were signs. We chose to ignore them.*

Carl reminded him so much of himself at that age. *The boy has real talent*, David thought. *There was no one there for me. It doesn't have to be the same with him.*

David's dream of becoming a famous writer crashed along with the launch of his one and only book. *They say that those that can, do. Those that can't, teach.* That worn out cliché that called him a failure droned though his mind for the last time. *Maybe it's time to call out that lie for what it is. A lie. Those that can, teach. That's what I do. Maybe it's time to consider this so-called plan of Mary's, or God's, or whomever's. Maybe I wasn't the one to become the famous novelist. Maybe I'm the one to create famous novelists. That's a real calling.*

David picked up a blank sheet of paper and started writing as Mary came out of the bedroom.

"What are you doing, hon?" she asked.

"Making a list," he replied.

"Oh, for the store?"

"No. A list of people I owe apologies." He kept on writing. *Carl Cook. Howard Bates, Deborah . . .*

"Why do you need to apologize?"

"Sit down. You missed a few things."

XIV

WAIT FOR the Lord; be strong, and let your heart take courage (Ps. 27:14).

Like a tornado destroying everything in its path, yet defied by one unlikely champion of hope, so this framed verse hung alone on the wall in the aftermath of a police search warrant. Carl's mother had embroidered it many years ago when hope seemed a real possibility. Despite all appearances to the contrary, she continued to believe to the end. Carl was still searching for a reason to believe. *Wait for what?* he wondered. *To be murdered?*

But waiting was over. Time had its chance. It failed. Now it was Carl's turn. That didn't mean that courage was a willing participant in his plan. No. That had to be dragged behind him across the kitchen floor of what was now considered a house of horrors and, at least for now, was his. *Maybe Detective Small was right,* he thought. *Maybe this wasn't such a good idea.*

He walked around flipping lights on, illuminating a panorama of helter-skelter. Not that the house hadn't already been in a state of decay. The police had just put the finishing touches on it.

"Sorry," said Detective Small walking in with a big wad of yellow police tape in his hand. "We'll fix it."

We? wondered Carl.

"Where's your waste basket?"

Carl spread his hands out over the floor covered in pots, pans, cooking utensils, silverware, and garbage.

"Uh . . . right," said the detective with an *oh yeah* look. "I'll find it."

Carl heard another car crunch up the gravel drive. He looked nervously out the window. *Who could this be?* Out stepped Eva Blankenship and Kathy Small in blue jeans and work boots. They started pulling some bags out of the back seat.

"The disaster relief crew," laughed the detective patting Carl on the back.

Relief crew? He watched as the two walked in. Their eyes opened wide. He expected them to make an about face and walk back out. They didn't.

"Oh, my," said Kathy giving him a shy smile and starting to unpack some cleaning supplies.

"You . . . you all are going to help?" squeaked Carl.

"Of course. That's what we're here for. By the way," said Kathy sheepishly, "I have to apologize for what happened at lunch. I was going to tell you who I was . . . but you know who," she said pointing her thumb at the detective, "had to show up and embarrass me."

The detective rolled his eyes.

"I know the feeling," replied Carl.

"Let's get started," said Luke. "Carl, you and I can put the furniture back in place and then work upstairs. The girls can clean up downstairs. Sound like a plan?"

"I'll get the kitchen cleaned up," said Eva, "and start some dinner."

Dinner?

Eva smiled. "You like spaghetti and meatballs?"

"No dinner from a can?" he replied under his breath. "Sure."

Kathy overheard him and laughed. "Where's the vacuum cleaner?"

Carl brought it out of the closet. Eva walked over to the sink and was taken aback by how deep and dirty the pile of dishes was. "Don't be hungry too soon," she sighed.

Luke and Carl went up the stairs as a cacophony of clinking dishes, clanging pots and whirring vacuum cleaner motors almost made the dead house seem alive.

It looked like a rabid poltergeist had satisfied its rage on the upstairs. His stepfather's room was particularly trashed, the mattress and box springs up against the wall, the bed disassembled in pieces, and all the dresser drawers dumped on the floor.

"Pretty thorough," remarked Carl.

"I'll do this one, Carl. It will give me one more chance to see if we missed anything."

"Yes, sir," replied Carl.

"Just call me Luke, Carl. You and I are going to be partners in this for some time." He held out his hand to shake on it.

Partners? "Yes, sir . . . I . . . uh mean, Luke," he replied shaking his hand.

Luke stood in the doorway. "Carl, you know the missing link right now is the murder weapon, we assume the bat. From all accounts, he treasured that thing. Is there any possibility he would have hid it somewhere in the house?"

Carl thought for a moment as an epiphany spread across his face. "Maybe," he said excitedly moving to the middle of the room where the bed had been. He knelt down and started knocking on the floor boards until one rang loose. He pulled it up revealing a cavity between the floor joists.

"I've seen him a couple times with his head under the bed," said Carl. "I assumed he was hiding drugs or something. He would get so angry when he saw me looking. I ducked away as quick as I could. I would hear the door slam shut behind me."

"Guess we weren't so thorough," replied Luke shaking his head. "Let's see what we have." He pulled out a pair of latex gloves and stretched them over his hands. "Always prepared," he said noticing Carl's curious eyes. "Hmmm . . . no bat, unfortunately, but what do we have here?"

He pulled out a plastic bag and a metal box.

"I remember that lock box!" exclaimed Carl. "My mother had it with her the night we were going to leave."

He dipped his little finger into a pouch of white powder. "Coke," he confirmed. "One more nail, but not enough to seal the coffin. Let's see what we have in here. Maybe this will help. Looks like the lock was pried open with a screwdriver or a pair of pliers. Carl, like I said. We're partners. This is evidence. Whatever we find, you have to keep to yourself. OK?"

Carl nodded as he watched the detective slowly lift the lid with an odd mixture of solemnity and the anticipation of a child about to open a surprise gift. Inside were a stack of papers, a roll of cash, and some photos. They sifted through the pictures, mostly of Carl growing up. Luke pulled out one old photo of a young couple with a newborn. Carl's face dropped.

"This guy looks about as happy as you," remarked the detective.

"My biological dad," replied Carl glumly. "Abandoned us. No need to worry about him."

"Understood," replied Luke. "We've all seen our share of hurt."

Carl looked over at him wondering what hurt he was talking about.

"Who is the woman standing beside them?"

"I don't know. I guess a friend."

Luke pulled out a bank statement and a cancelled check. The account had been closed October 27, 2015, two days before her supposed murder. The check was in the amount of the balance of about thirty nine thousand dollars and some change. "Looks like she was prepared financially to leave," said the detective. He counted the roll of money. Less than ten thousand dollars. "I wonder where the rest of it is."

"I think it's called a Ford F–150 4x4," replied Carl. "It's not on the house or on me."

"I'll bet you're right, Carl. We're getting closer."

He pulled out a copy of her life insurance policy. Someone had scribbled a number and a name on it. Then he pulled out a deed. "This is your mother's house, Carl. No other name on the deed." Then he pulled out a Last Will and Testament and read it over quickly. "And now it's yours according to this. Guess we know why he didn't put it up as security for bond."

The other papers included social security documents, passports, two marriage certificates, a divorce certificate, and two birth certificates. Carl saw the detective freeze as he held up both birth certificates. The suspense built to a crescendo as he studied the documents.

"What is it?" asked Carl.

"Look at this."

He laid the two on the floor side by side. They were identical except the names were different. *I can't believe he is showing me all this*, thought Carl.

Carl's head oscillated from one to the other. Same hospital. Same date. "What's this mean? Who is this other boy?" he asked the detective.

"That's a good question. I have an idea, Carl, but before I say, I need Sarah to check some information first."

"What have you guys been doing?" demanded Eva standing over them. "The downstairs is about done."

Carl and Luke looked like they had been caught by a Warrant Officer.

"Uh, well my junior detective and I have been detecting," Luke replied in defense.

"Some detecting. You didn't even hear me coming. But, if that worked you up an appetite, better get to the table while it's hot," she countered turning on her heel.

They act like they're married, thought Carl, or how he imagined normal married people acted.

"I say we get down there, Carl. Hungry?"

"Yes, sir," he agreed. Satisfying his stomach was one thing, but these mysteries were working up another appetite. That would take more time to satisfy.

"I'll meet you down there. I need to go grab some evidence bags first."

Everyone waited for Luke to crisscross the kitchen to the car, to the bedroom, back to the car, and finally to the table. The small talk was filled with a strange familiarity. It seemed as if the three of them were a family. In a stranger way, Carl felt like he belonged though he had no claim. He was confused.

"Dad says we almost have the same birthday, Carl," said Kathy.

"Oh?"

"Yeah. Almost. I was born just a few minutes after midnight. Missed you by a day."

"Wow. We just found another . . ."

"Carl," said Luke with his finger up to his lips. "Loose lips . . . you know."

"Right. Sorry."

"So, big secret," she laughed. "I bet you're excited about getting a driver's license. I know I am."

"Really. Yeah, me too. I guess I've been too distracted lately. With my newfound independence, I'm going to have to figure a way to get over to the DMV and find a car to road test in."

"No problem. Dad will take us both. Right, Daddy?" she said looking over at her father with a time tested little girl smile.

"I don't want to be a burden," intervened Carl.

"It's not a burden, Carl. I would be happy to take you," said Luke looking at his daughter with mock scorn. "I would have done it without being called Daddy."

Carl watched the three of them start to laugh and then found himself joining in. A strange feeling spread over him like a warm blanket on a cold night.

"Thanks . . . for everything," said Carl.

"You're welcome, Carl. And Kathy and I will be taking you to and from school for a while until we finish this investigation. I still don't like the idea of you being out here alone." He looked at Carl with a stern look more akin to that of a caring father. At least that is how Carl perceived it. It was another new feeling.

After dinner, they finished the upstairs. "One last thing, Carl," said the detective. "Let's put this board back. Tomorrow, we have to let your stepfather back to retrieve his belongings." He winked as he got on his hands and knees, placed the board back in place and inserted a small matchstick in the crack. Carl's eyes lit up with a knowing expression.

As they left, Luke gave some final instructions. "You may see a car roll past here every couple hours or so. That will be one of my officers, not Wickes. If you see anything, and I mean anything, strange or doesn't seem right, you call me immediately and 9–1–1. Don't wait. You have a cell phone with my number. It's on speed dial."

"Yes, sir."

When it came time to say goodbye, Eva and Kathy each gave him a tight hug. He didn't want to let go. Luke squeezed him around the shoulders.

As their taillights disappeared into the night, another unfamiliar pang emerged in the pit of his stomach. It was homesickness, but for a home he had never seen. Maybe it was the one his mother had waited for.

XV

SOME TEACH others to fish. Some give others a fish. Some just fish. Principal Nick Thompson stared at the six pound trophy brown trout mounted on a shiny shellacked oak plaque that flew proudly over his credenza as if it were second only to bagging Big Foot. The tiny #16 White Sulphur Dun that brought down this mighty fish dripped off its lip.

The last morning bell had rung, the announcements were made and all the little piggies were in their pens. He pulled out an LL Bean catalog out of his lap drawer as he dreamed of where his next conquest would take him. A new set of stocking foot waders was imminent, size XXL. He tugged on his belt but it slid back down like his belly had been greased. Unfazed, he leaned back and stuffed the other half of a raspberry jelly donut in his mouth and washed it down with lukewarm sugar laden coffee.

He used the point of his pencil to flip the page on his desk calendar which had become nothing more than a paper abacus counting down to the end of the school year. The light was glowing brighter each day as he neared the end of dealing with ungrateful urchins full of hormonal rages and stroking teachers whose egos had become too big to wrap your arms around. Thirty years was enough. He deserved a rest. He would take his hoary head and spend it wading the back streams of Maine.

He jerked as his placid reverie was dissipated by the crackling intercom. It was like receiving an electric shock each time. "Mr. Thompson, your appointment is here."

"Thank you, Patti. Please send him in." He quickly hid the catalog and waited for the door to open.

Patti opened the door ushering in Detective Luke Small. The detective considered himself of average height and stature, but when Principal Thompson walked around the desk that diminutive feeling grabbed him like a vise as the large man towered above. It was like standing in the shadow of Grizzly Adams, beard and all.

"Mr. Thompson, pleased to meet you," he said.

"Pleased to meet you, Detective. Can I get you a coffee? Donut?" he asked, pointing to the plate of jelly donuts on his desk.

The detective patted his own belly. "Thanks, but no. I certainly suffer enough from those occupational hazards, you know. And reap the consequences."

They both chuckled nervously. "Please have a seat," said the principal.

As detectives do, he looked around to get a sense of the man in front of him. "That is some fish," he said pointing to the trophy. "You must be quite a fisherman."

"Well," he said, hiding his pride about as well as the emperor hid his new clothes, "I might have been lucky or maybe he was just unlucky."

"Nevertheless, I hope to get that lucky now that I'm up here."

"I did hear you were from away. I can definitely help out a city boy when it comes to navigating the woods of Maine. Just let me know when you are ready."

"Thanks," replied the detective to the rhetorical offer. "My wife was a native if that makes me less from away."

"Sorry, Detective. No credit for that," he laughed. "Tell me, what can I do for you? When I got your call, I must say I was kind of curious how Woodspring High School could help you."

"Well, I won't take up much of your time. I wanted to talk to you and maybe some of your teachers. As we investigate the murder of Susan Cook, we are trying to find out as much as we can about the family. You know . . . her, Kevin, Carl, and any other significant others that dealt with the family. How well did you know the Cooks?"

"Actually, none at all. I know they lived out of town a ways. I don't recall Kevin ever coming to the high school. I believe Susan may have been here once during a parent–teachers conference, but with so many parents, I really don't have a recollection of who comes and who doesn't."

"I see. What about Carl? What kind of a student is he?"

"There again, not much, which as a high school principal is a good thing. The ones I know well, you don't want to know. Of course, with the news of his mother, I have been paying more attention. I understand he is a decent student, a bit of a loner, stays to himself, and doesn't seek attention in any of the wrong ways. Wish I had a few hundred more of him," he said with a half laugh.

"I see. I have his school records here," Detective Small said pulling a manila file out of his valise. "Let's see . . . it looks like his freshman year started out very well, dipped about midterm and then gradually improved over the course of the remaining school year. Any opinion on that?"

"Hmmm . . . no, not really," he replied taking a thoughtful posture. "I don't think he was an overly ambitious student. Sometimes their interest can vary a lot depending on what they are studying at that time, or the level of hormones if you know what I mean. I have heard he was entirely capable of having high grades in all of his classes."

"Well, there seems to be a specific time we can point at, possibly an event in his life that had some emotional distress. I would say about this time last year. It was about the time his mother disappeared and also he was severely injured. Do you remember any of those events?"

"No . . . no. No one reported anything like that to me. I wasn't aware his mother was missing and no one reported any physical injuries."

"Were you aware of Carl coming to school with any other injuries either last school year or this one?"

Principal Thompson started fidgeting in his seat. "No, Detective. I can't say that I was aware."

"What about last Friday? Carl showed up with a swollen face. Did anyone make you aware of this?"

"No. No one did," he replied. "Is there a reason for these questions?"

"Actually, yes. As principal, you know it is mandated in the State of Maine for teachers, guidance counselors, school officials, school bus drivers, and the like . . . here, let me read it to you." He pulled some more papers out of his valise and continued, ". . . such persons, it says, shall immediately report or cause a report to be made to the department when the person knows or has reasonable cause to suspect that a child has been or is likely to be abused or neglected or that a suspicious child death has occurred."

"I know that," said the principal sitting more erect. "So? Your point?"

The detective could feel the principal's intimidation factor chiming it. It was no doubt a necessary and effective tool for handling teachers and students, but was about to fall flat on the detective.

"The point, Mr. Thompson," replied the detective mirroring his tone, "is that Carl Cook has shown up at this school numerous times with injuries that should have provoked enough interest for someone to delve into how they occurred. Has all your staff been trained in how to spot and report such abuse?"

"Of course, Detective Small. Maybe you should talk to his guidance counselor, Mrs. Adkins."

"I did. I got the same answers. Seems no one is aware of anything out of the ordinary."

"Well, there you go. Apparently there was nothing to report."

"Well, not necessarily. Mrs. Adkins had never met with Carl, didn't even know who he was until she opened his file."

"Well, I'm sorry we couldn't help you more, Detective," said the principal rising from his chair as if on cue, "but we can't make up answers you want to hear. Perhaps you should talk to Principal Delgado at the Junior High School. I would think he would have more history on this student than we."

"Actually, I did talk to Mr. Delgago," said the detective staying in his seat. "He also doesn't seem to recollect any particular symptoms of abuse either. Boys will be boys was all he had to say."

"Maybe that's because that is all it is," the principal said as his cheeks turned a brighter shade of pink and his clenched knuckles a whiter shade of white.

"Actually, maybe not, Mr. Thompson. Anyway," he said getting up from his chair and collecting his papers, "I've taken up enough of your time. There is one teacher I would like to chat with for a few moments, if possible."

"Whatever you need," replied the principal walking to the door. "Who would you like to talk to?"

Detective Small looked down at his notepad. "Mr. Howard Bates. I think he might have had contact with Carl outside of school, like church."

The principal opened up a ring binder on his desk and ran his finger down the page. "Looks like I can free up Mr. Bates this period for you if you are ready."

"That would be great, Mr. Thompson," he said shaking the principal's huge moist hand.

"It was nice meeting you, Detective." He leaned out the door. "Patti, would you please escort Detective Small to the conference room and send a message to Mr. Bates that the detective would like to chat with him?"

"Yes, sir," she replied.

"And come back to my office when you're done."

"Yes, sir."

Principal Thompson closed the door, walked over to his desk and threw the remaining donuts into the trash. He took another check of his desk calendar. One hundred and twenty five more days. Not soon enough.

Patti Pearson returned a few minutes later.

"Have a seat, Patti, and take a memo. To all teachers and staff. The subject line will be Mandatory Training – Maine Statute – Title 22 – Mandatory Reporting of Abuse and Neglect."

§§§

Howard Bates had one of those Cheshire cat smiles ubiquitous with TV preachers that he was sure couldn't be cracked if they were standing in front of firing squad. Luke always looked for the eyes. They were the giveaway.

"Nice to meet you, officer," said Howard as he walked in the conference room with his hand stuck out ten feet away.

Detective Small didn't bother to correct him. "Thanks for taking the time to talk to me," he replied.

"How can I help you?" asked Howard enthusiastically taking a seat across from the detective.

"As I'm sure you know, I'm investigating the Susan Cook murder . . ."

"Such a tragedy," he said shaking his head and losing the smile.

"Yes. Anyway, I understand you were the deacon for the Cook family?"

"Yes, I was."

"What can you tell me about them? I assume you knew Kevin, Susan, and Carl."

"I can't really say much about Kevin. He stopped coming to church . . . let's see . . . several years ago I guess. Susan and Carl were very faithful up until, I guess, a year ago. Then I heard she had left town."

"You were born and raised here in Woodspring, correct?" asked the detective.

"I was," replied Howard.

"So, it's a small town. You must know something about Kevin other than through the church."

Howard thought for a second. "Sure, but nothing worth repeating. There is always a lot of gossip, but I stay out of it."

"So you know nothing of his reputation? Whether he was a drunk? Or a violent man?"

"Again," replied Howard, "I don't repeat gossip."

That's pretty righteous, thought the detective. *I'll bet you're all ears though.* "I see. Can you tell me more about Susan? As her deacon, did she ever confide in you about issues or problems at home, with her husband for instance?"

"Not really. Pastor Glenn took care of spiritual counseling. Before that, I know she talked to Pastor Theriault. I know she was just a faithful Christian lady. She gave her tithes and offerings each week. A model Christian."

That's all it takes, I guess. "It doesn't sound like you spent a lot of time with her or her family?"

"Well, the church has taken a different direction since our new pastor came a couple years ago. Our mission is more focused on growing membership. You know, to make more disciples for Christ."

"So how did that impact the disciples you already had?" asked the detective.

Howard's eyes narrowed. "I'm not sure I understand your question."

"Forget it. Let's talk about Carl. You also have him for math? How is he doing?"

"Wonderful kid. Very smart. He does seem to vary a bit in his interest and grades."

"Did you ever discuss with him why they might vary?"

"No. I kind of assume that's our guidance counselor's job."

"Wouldn't you as a deacon, get personally involved?"

"Well, we are trained to separate the two, you know, church and state." Apparently the direction of the detective's questioning was more effective than facing a firing squad. The teacher's smile started to crack.

"OK, not your job. We can handle them separately. Here at school, tell me, did you ever see evidence of child abuse or neglect?"

Again, Howard took a thoughtful mien. "No . . . I can't say that I have," he answered but his eyes told a different story.

"Were you ever trained on the mandatory reporting of abuse and neglect and how to identify patterns?"

Howard's face went into recall mode as he twisted his mustache. "I was," he said. "I think it was part of our orientation as teachers."

"And how long has that been?"

Howard gave a faint laugh. "Well, I've been here for over twenty years."

The detective tried his best not to roll his eyes.

"OK, then let's switch gears to church. How about when his mother allegedly left town? Carl was left behind. Did Carl not come to church because he no longer wished to or because he had no transportation or some other reason?"

Howard fumbled for an answer. "I must admit, I'm not sure. We were so focused on our main mission."

Main mission? thought the detective. *What am I missing here? No more tithes and offerings?* "So no one cared enough to check on him?"

"Of course we cared," replied Howard, the remnants of any smile completely breaking ranks. "We do a lot of good things!"

"I'm sure. I didn't mean to offend you. Back here to school. You say no one noticed any abuse. Yet recently, Carl showed up to school with half of his face bashed in. No one noticed that?"

"He said he ran into a door," replied Howard starting to fight back.

"And you believed that? Don't you know from your training that abused children will often try to cover up the truth for fear of their abusers?"

"Again, Officer, that training was a long time ago."

"Detective," said the detective. "Not officer."

"What?"

"Nothing. OK, Mr. Bates. I thank you for your time. I think I have all I need for now."

Howard stood up. He wiped a drop of sweat from his brow. "Anytime."

They shook hands. Howard turned and closed the door behind him.

Detective Small looked at his notes and then up at the ceiling. *They say it takes a village to raise a child, but apparently not on this planet.*

XVI

EVERYONE WAKES up in the middle of the night remembering something they forgot to do, such as did they leave the burners on, leave the windows open, let the cat in, or pay that bill? Few wake up wondering what they did with the murder weapon.

Kevin Cook's head slumped darkly over a mug of beer in the darkest corner of a dark bar called Barb's Deepwoods Saloon. Deepwoods was as far off the grid as its name implied, frequented by lumber jacks, mountain men, and biker clubs. It smelled of beer, whiskey, urine and vomit. The bartender, proprietor, and chief bottle washer had a sawed off shotgun under the counter. Barbara was no virgin to its use.

His mind, what little he could activate, was freewheeling like a log rolling in the river and going nowhere. What had he done with the bat? He remembered Charley handing him the bat. He had told him to burn it and had even stoked up the fire to get it hot enough before he left. He told him not to drink anymore. It wasn't easy to part with. It also wasn't easy to stay away from that last bottle of Jim Beam he had hidden under the counter. The last thing he remembered was sitting on the floor with the bat and a bottle of whiskey.

How do I tell Charley? he asked himself. *Should I tell him? Maybe I did burn it.* The more he thought about it, the surer he was that he had complied with the order. Or did he?

"What are you thinking about?" He looked up to see Charley take a seat in the booth opposite Kevin.

"Well . . . uh . . . you know. A bunch of stuff."

Charley nodded. "Did you get your things?"

"Yeah."

"Missing anything?"

"Yeah," he replied without looking up.

"Yeah is right. You now have another charge. Drug possession."

"I figured. And they got all the cash I had left."

"Well, I can't help you with that after posting bail. And I can't have you staying with me either, obviously."

"I'll hole up at Mack's until I can figure something out."

"If you can stand the smell."

"Guess I'll have to. So, you're the legal expert. How bad is this thing looking? What do they really have? You can't believe anything they say. They're all a bunch of liars."

"Everyone is scared to talk to me about the case. They're scared of this Small. The Chief likes him a lot. No one seems able to size him up. Munson in evidence is the only one talking. That's how I learned about the coke."

"Anything else?" he asked knowing the answer was about to be rubbed in his face.

"Oh, yeah," he replied dryly. "Susan's personal papers. Last Will and Testament. Deed. Life insurance policy. Bank account. You should have burned all of that along with the bat. What possessed you to hold on to that stuff?"

"I don't know. Stupid, I guess."

"Forest Gump's words ring true all right. Stupid is as stupid does," Charley said, his contorted face making no attempt to hide his fury. "You're getting me deep in the thick of this, you idiot!"

"Sorry," said Kevin staring at his beer.

"Sorry isn't going to save either of us," Charley said.

"I know. Are they going to make a murder charge?"

"I don't know. They probably have enough to indict, at least on manslaughter."

"Then why don't they?"

"Because they don't want to lose and there is a chance they could. Law enforcement has the patience of Job when it comes to stuff like this. They own the time."

"Wonderful."

"OK, let's go over everything one more time. It's the details that nail everyone that gets convicted. I'm hanging out there as much as you are, thanks to your . . . whatever. We're good on the cleanup. They found no DNA or blood evidence. Let's start with the car. Mack was going to bury it in the woods."

Kevin was silent.

"Ohhhh . . . don't tell me," said Charley, his impatience starting to make sounds like a tea kettle reaching the boiling point.

"Well, I'm not sure. He was talking about a chop shop he knew in Kentucky. Said he needed the money and that it would never be traced. I was just glad he took it."

"Glad, huh?" said Charley his face looking more like Satan's than human. "Needed the money, huh? He was paid. Details,

Kevin. Look at me. Details. You have to know everything. You can't assume. We'll find out about the car. What about the bat. That is the one thing that ends it all for both of us. Blood. Fingerprints. Everything they need. You burned it that night, right?"

Kevin didn't answer.

"Right?" demanded Charley. "What's it take to get a straight answer out of you?"

"I think so . . . yes . . . I did."

Charley's face boiled to a lobster red as his rage let loose with unmitigated wrath. "You think?" yelled Charley.

Barbara reached her tattooed arm under the counter and rapped the famous mediator on the bar. Charley took notice.

"You think so," he continued in a whisper. "What's that mean? My fingerprints were on that bat too. If that shows up, we're both toast. You idiot."

"Wait . . . wait," said Kevin, his lips quivering, "don't get upset. I'm sure I burned it. It's . . . it's just that I don't remember."

"What do you mean you don't remember? How can you not remember every single detail of that night?" His eyes rolled toward the ceiling as it dawned on him. He looked over at Barbara who watched them like a prison guard. "Don't tell me you had another bottle laid away?"

"Look," Kevin continued his pitiful defense, "it was gone in the morning. I'm sure I burned it . . . and then, you know, well . . . I guess I passed out. Don't worry. It's gone."

"Right," he sneered. "I won't worry. And what about Carl. I can't get access to his testimony. He was gone when I got there. Just how much did he see?"

"He didn't see the end."

"But he saw you hitting her, right? Did he see you with the bat?"

Kevin's hesitating answers did nothing but fuel Charley's already charged anger.

"Well?" he demanded.

"He may have seen me with the bat . . . but not hit her."

Charley took a breath, tilted his head back and stared at the ceiling as if waiting for some dark angel from the other side to give him an answer. "OK . . . calm down," he said more to clear the cotton out of his own head than concern for Kevin's fear. "OK . . . is there any, and I mean any possibility, no matter how remote it might be, that you hid that bat anywhere in the house?

That in your drunkenness you might have tried to save it but just don't remember?"

Kevin's last hesitation was too much. Charley tried to satisfy his rage by grabbing his shirt collar and almost pulling him across the table. He released his grip as Barbara rapped that shotgun on the counter one more time. There was no third time. After that, the mediator would execute its judgment.

"Maybe," replied Kevin as all the courage drained from his face. "There were a few other places I used to hide stuff. But I didn't get a chance. That officer they sent with me . . . uh . . ."

"Chris Blaise," said Charley finishing his sentence. "A Boy Scout."

"Yeah . . . him. He watched me like a hawk. I only had a chance to check my bedroom. For some reason he gave me some privacy in there."

"He did, huh?" said Charley. "Interesting."

"So, what do you think, Charley?" asked Kevin in an attempt to shunt Charley's anger. "What do we do now?"

Charley's face went through a series of contortions and chin rubbing until it finally mellowed out. There was only one answer.

"There are only two things that could really bury us," said Charley. "The bat if it still exists . . ." He paused as if to choose his words carefully. "Would have to be in the house somewhere."

"And?"

"And? Are you serious?" replied Charley as he wished he could at least have a moron for a partner in crime. "What do you think? The kid!"

"So, what are we going to do?"

Charley wagged his head. "They have to go. The house. The kid. Anything that can be used as evidence against us. You worried about either?"

"No. The house ain't mine. And he ain't blood. Just a bastard kid."

"OK, then."

"How?" asked Kevin.

Charley looked at Kevin knowing the entire weight of this operation rested on him. "Mack."

XVII

IT IS written, *Do not lay up for yourselves treasures on earth, where moth and rust destroy and where thieves break in and steal, but lay up for yourselves treasures in heaven, where neither moth nor rust destroys and where thieves do not break in and steal. For where your treasure is, there your heart will be also.*

Perry Richardson was a rich man. Wealth was something he neither feared nor loved. It just was. He was surrounded by many earthly treasures but the only one that mattered was like a vapor that appeared for a short time and then vanished away. Knowing that she was in heaven provided solace somewhere in that hidden part of him, but did little to blunt the feelings of loss.

There were so many whys. *Did I love her too much? Did I put her ahead of God? Is that why He took her?* Deborah said he fooled her at Yale. The confident look wasn't because of his wealth. It was because of the confidence of his faith. That is what drew her to him. She would laugh and call him her camel who threaded the eye of the needle that had denied so many other rich men entry to heaven.

Where is that faith now? he asked himself. *The one that could call those things that be not as though they are, the substance of things hoped for, the evidence of things not seen. Where is it now, God?* His brain kept running until it finally keeled over as if it had just completed a marathon. It couldn't go another mile. *It's God's plan, not mine.* He would know some day.

The rapping on the door got louder and louder until it finally returned him to the present. "Come in."

"Here is the file you asked for, Perry."

Perry slowly reached for the file as if he were getting ready to press two hundred pounds.

"Are you all right, Perry?" she asked.

Perry stared at the file like he hadn't heard her.

"Sir?"

"Oh . . . sorry, Robin. Thank you. Guess I'm out of it today."

Robin turned to leave but stopped at the doorway. "Sir, we . . . I mean the staff and I are so sorry." She stood there as if wanting to say more but the words would not come.

Perry looked up at her as if she had just appeared. "I appreciate that, Robin. Thank you."

As she started to close the door he said, "Wait, Robin. If you don't mind. Do you have a minute?"

"Of course. What do you need?"

"Uh . . . I don't know. Have a seat."

Perry continued to stare at the unopened file in silence for a full minute before speaking. Finally he said, "Deb was always my sounding board on these cases, you know." He cracked a weak smile. "Guess you just got promoted."

"Certainly, sir. Anything you need," she said stiffening her back as if to take dictation. "Of course, I'm only a paralegal."

"Don't shortchange yourself. We have enough legal gurus working the angles. What we need is a little more empathy." He pointed at the file. "You and I have sure worked a lot of these personal injury cases."

"We certainly have," she agreed leaning forward.

"We have seen some really bad things happen to people. Things that demanded action. But I have to confess, we . . . I mean me . . . I tell them how sorry I am, how we are going to get them justice . . . that they deserve the most we can get . . . but the truth is there never is a real connection with the victim. It's something that happened to them . . . someone else . . . not me. They might be sitting right in front of me. I might be patting them on the arm. Don't get me wrong. There is some feeling but it's like . . . how would you say . . . hugging someone without actually touching them. I can relate in part but only in part to their pain or loss. Do you know what I mean?"

"I do," she said, her face mirroring his pain. "I know. It's different. We loved her too. The whole team is feeling it."

"Thank you," he said looking down at his desk. "It's hard to explain."

They both stared into space for a couple minutes.

"You know another thing," he continued, "all the money in the world can't heal either. With so many of our clients it's just been about the money. As a disclaimer, I have to charge us with the same motive . . . after all, this is the business we are in. But at the end of the day, the healing doesn't begin or end because of a million dollar award. It rings hollow."

Robin pointed at his file. "What are we going do about this one? If anyone deserves to pay, she does."

"Maybe so. She was ninety years old. Shouldn't have been driving. But no. We are not going to file suit. There has been enough blood shed. She will probably never see the outside of a hospital. That will be the start of my healing. Take whatever settlement the insurance company offers and give it to Deb's favorite charity, St. Jude's Leukemia Foundation."

Robin reached over and touched his arm. "I will."

"Robin, you were pretty close to Deb. Can I share some private things with you?"

"Of course, Perry. You can tell me anything."

"Deb had secrets, but she hid them in plain sight. She told me they were all in her diary, right there in her desk drawer. It seemed like she was almost inviting me to find out for myself so she wouldn't have to tell me. She said that she would share them in due time and I respected that. It was something that troubled her for many years. Maybe I should have forced it. Time ran out. Maybe I could have helped her."

Robin leaned forward as if trying to console him on some ethereal level.

"The diary only covered about a year and a half, her freshman year at Orono. She was fresh off the farm, so to speak. Not exactly off the farm, but I loved to tease her like that. She would get so feisty and defensive. Anyway, that has nothing to do with the story. Sorry. In a nutshell, when she was a freshman she fell in love . . . got pregnant . . . decided not to tell her mother . . . and put the baby up for adoption. And that is where her entries end . . . at the birth. She never wrote another word in that diary other than a letter to me at the end as if knowing how it would all go. She just locked it up in her heart and carried it alone all these years."

"Oh, dear," she said. "What a burden to carry." She could feel the weight in Perry's eyes.

"Yes. A burden she shouldn't have carried alone. I don't judge the decisions she made. She had her reasons. But now we know these children exist . . ."

"Children?"

Perry smiled. "Yes. If you can believe it. She had twins. A boy and a girl. Just like Jess and Bess. I have to find out where they are . . . to make sure they're OK."

"What do you need me to do?" asked Robin.

"I don't know where to start. About a year ago she made a personal trip to Memphis. Do you remember? Maybe there was something to that."

"I do remember. I asked her what she was going for since it wasn't the typical business trip. She seemed unusually excited for someone who hated to travel. I received a one word answer– redemption. She said it with conviction and a smile on her face and turned and walked off. I was puzzled but oddly happy for her."

"Redemption? Maybe it's a clue. There were some unusual disbursements from her account shortly after . . ."

"Mr. Richardson, you have a call." Perry cringed as the intercom blasted him in mid-sentence.

He reached over and reduced the volume. "Who is it, Donna? I'm in a meeting. I asked to take messages except for emergencies."

"That's what I told her. She said she had some information for you that you would want to hear immediately."

"Who is it?" he asked impatiently.

"It's a Ms. Elizabeth Mills . . . calling from Maine."

Perry's eyes lit up. "I'll take it."

Robin got up to leave.

"No, stay," he said gesturing for her to sit back down

Perry put it on the speaker phone.

"Hi, Liz. How are you? How is Skowhegan?"

"Hi, Perry. I'm doing fine. Cold will be the stock answer for the next few months."

Perry laughed. "Well, I won't tell you what it is here," he replied. "By the way, I have you on the speaker phone with my paralegal, Robin Peters."

"That is fine. Hi, Robin," she said.

"Hi, Ms. Mills," she replied.

"Anyway," she said continuing. "I told you I couldn't remember what the name of the adoption agency was that Deborah used. I climbed up in the attic and found some old photos and papers. It was Les Enfants in Bangor. They specialized in newborns. I remember the people there. They were so nice."

"Wonderful. So they have the records?" asked Perry.

"They do. I went ahead and made a call. The president is still Nathan Bourassa. He and his wife, Sally run it. They remember Deborah, you know, the surprise of twins and all. But the adoption papers are sealed. You know more about that kind of stuff than I do. They said the only way to get them unsealed is for a close relative to have a court order issued. I guess that falls to you."

"Hmmm . . . I think we can handle that," he said winking at Robin. "Let me get on it. Don't worry. We will find them. I'll be sure to keep you in the loop. I can't thank you enough."

"Oh, it's my pleasure. Anything for you and Deborah. You just let me know. Good bye."

"Good bye, Liz. And thanks again."

"How fortuitous," he said smiling at Robin, "that we just had this conversation."

"I'm on it, Perry," she said and was out the door in a flash.

XVIII

MAINE, IT is said, is the way life should be. That opinion could vary on a moment by moment basis as Luke Small was learning snaking his way up Route 201 toward Jackman. November was an ugly duckling phase between Fall and Winter. Enough snow had fallen the night before to elegantly dress the pines in glistening white gowns, but now it was melting and throwing up a stew of salt and crud on his windshield with each logging truck he met, and he met quite a few.

Thoughts of the case nagged him like unwelcome backseat drivers as trees whipped by him on both sides as if driving through a movie set. So little was known about the victim. She wasn't local. She had been married at least once before. Maybe the man in the photograph he and Carl had found was his biological father, but that was not certain. One thing that was certain was that Susan was not his biological mother. DNA had eliminated that possibility. But he needed more answers before telling Carl who would have plenty of questions of his own.

Susan had been the bookkeeper for Morris Lumber. Dick Morris seemed to be closer to her than anyone so far but even what he knew was sketchy. He remarked on her excellent work. She was very much an introvert but would open up at times if she thought anyone was interested in her story. She majored in finance at UMO but quit her senior year. She never said why. It was clear her life revolved around Carl. She talked about him all the time. He was going to be a famous author, she said with her characteristic confidence. Dick was upset when she "left town" as was reported. There was no one that could replace her. When he heard the news that her body had been found, he shut the plant down and sent everyone home with pay.

Why would anyone quit their senior year, he wondered, *when they were so close to getting a degree? That doesn't make sense. There's a story here somewhere.* He hoped to find some answers in Jackman. The only other person who might shed more light was the retired Pastor Joseph Theriault, at least according to a few parishioners. They said they seemed very close. She and he had many private meetings. Some were even bold enough to suggest an illicit relationship, but of course didn't want to initiate any rumormongering.

Luke passed the *Welcome to Jackman* sign and turned onto Rt. 6 toward Long Pond and then realized he wasn't sure where he was going. No GPS was going to help him from this point on. He pulled over and grabbed the directions off the passenger seat. Gravel road, two miles, dirt road.

"Where's that four wheel drive I requested now," he grumbled, "when I need it?"

He looked at his watch. It was close to noon. He wondered if he should grab lunch somewhere or if there even was a somewhere. There was the Mountainview resort back along the road but he wasn't sure if they had a restaurant. Backtracking could be a waste of time. *Let's just get this done*, he decided and turned up the second gravel road on the right. After about a couple miles there was the sign he was looking for nailed to a spruce: *The Theriault's*. He turned up the pine passageway. He could hear mud caking up against the rocker panels. Finally a modest cabin came into view. The cedar shake siding had clearly danced with more than a few Maine winters. The lake behind the cabin was like a huge shimmering mirror that duplicated the gorgeous Maine wilderness dressed in white. *Now that is the way life should be*, he affirmed. A canopy jutted out from the right side of the house covering a few cords of hardwood. A white plume spiraled curlicue letters out of the chimney sending smoke signals in the still blue sky to anyone who could read them. A blue Ford Bronco with a rusted tailgate was parked under another canopy on the left side. Luke pulled up, parked, and grabbed his notebook.

The door opened before he could knock. "Detective Small, I presume," greeted a thin old man with an engaging smile of ragtag teeth. "Please, come in. It's cold out there don't ya know."

"Thank you, Pastor," said Luke as the man took his hand and practically pulled him in.

"Ain't no pastor around here," he laughed. "Call me Joe." He took Luke's trench coat and hung it on a hat rack of deer antlers. He could feel the warmth radiating across the room from the wood stove. "I made us up a little lunch, Detective. I figured you might be hungry making the trek up this far into the woods."

"Please, call me Luke. You didn't need to do that," he said as he mentally questioned his policy of not imposing during interviews, but only for a second. "But now that you mention it."

"Please make yourself comfortable. I'll be right back."

As the reverend went into the kitchen, Luke made his usual visual rounds. There were several old and newer photos on the mantel. Most seemed to be of family, presumably his wife, children, and grandchildren telling the tale of a full life. The walls resembled more the Museum of Natural History. There were a couple large fish mounted, what kind he didn't know, a twelve point buck, a moose head, and a black bear skin that was stretched on the wall like a shadow about to attack. Surprisingly, there were almost no religious trappings except for one framed poster of a long elaborate banquet table that seemingly went on to infinity. The inscription read, *Come For All Things Are Ready*. He scanned his library, a place that usually held telling signs. It had a variety of well used books, mostly titles dealing with Christianity, deeper life, and Christian mystics, all of them foreign to Luke. There were a few on fishing and hunting.

Joe returned with two paper plates loaded with ham and cheese sandwiches and chips and placed them on the coffee table. "Sit down over there, Luke," he said pointing to a well broken–in armchair. "What would you like to drink? Tea? Water? Coffee? Ah . . . I can see it in your eyes," he laughed. "Me too. I'm guessing, black?"

"The only way," smiled Luke sinking deeply into the cushions, "straight up." He already liked this guy and his chair. *I'm going to need some coffee if I sit in this thing very long.*

"I agree."

"This is a very nice place," Luke said when Joe returned.

"It has a lot of memories. More for the kids. These are monuments to their manhood on the wall," he said pointing around. "But it works for me. I sold our place in Woodspring after my wife passed. It's a great place to do my writing."

"Sorry. I heard about your wife."

"Thanks. We're OK. It's all part of life."

Tell me about it, thought Luke. "Say, did I notice your name on one of the books in your library?"

"Wow, you are a detective, Luke. Oh, there might be one or two of my bestsellers in there. And I've got a ton of them in the loft to prove it," he said with a hearty laugh. "I'll give you a copy before you leave."

"Thanks." *He sure laughs a lot.*

"Sorry about the simple fare, but the menus aren't quite the same anymore."

"Maybe we can share recipes. I've been a widower myself for four years now."

"Oh, I'm sorry to hear that. You're so young. Sickness?"

"Cancer."

"That is so devastating, I know," he said nodding. "Those are times when it's difficult to see God's love."

See God's love? That immediately ignited a flashback to his knockdown drag out with God. He brought himself back. He was a professional. But he wasn't done with God. The next round would have to wait.

"Uh . . . yeah, Reverend. It was difficult seeing the love of God anywhere." He took a bite of his sandwich. "I don't want to take up too much of your time, so I guess we can talk while we eat," he said racing away from the topic.

The reverend looked at his watch. "Got nothing but time," he laughed.

"I met your successor," Luke said. "He was interesting. I don't know if it's the right thing to say about a pastor, but he seems to be on the fast track of something."

"That's probably appropriate," said Joe. "Very charismatic. Probably a mile wide and an inch deep."

"I think I had the same sentiments, just didn't put it so eloquently. You and I, I think, are in the same business when it comes to sizing up people."

"True," agreed the pastor.

"How did you feel about him taking the helm? They say there were a lot of changes. They even changed the name of the church."

"Well, the winds of change were starting to blow before he came on board. Some of deacons, particularly the younger ones, felt that just preaching Christ wasn't enough. Membership wasn't increasing so something had to be wrong. Everything is driven by metrics these days. Unfortunately, spiritual maturity isn't so easy to measure. Membership is. They wanted to attract a broader audience so they decided to rebrand. They found a pastor trained in the latest management techniques that would increase, in their parlance, market share."

"I guess it worked," commented Luke.

"Not really," responded Joe. "I mean I don't say that out of envy or dejection that they have increased membership. The increase in numbers does not necessarily equate to an increase in the number of believers, if you know what I mean."

"That doesn't sound good," said Luke detecting some heaviness in his words.

"It may seem counterintuitive, but God is always there if you know where to look. You can't thwart His kingdom no matter how hard you try. They will try and fail. Failure is a good thing. Then they will return to the gospel."

"I'll take your word for that. Relating that to the topic at hand, it does seem like they neglected some things that might have been, at least in my opinion, more important. Like their existing members. Like Susan Cook and Carl Cook. It's like they dropped right off the rolls."

Joe nodded. "I'm sure. It may not seem right or fair, but God is working in that situation also."

Luke looked up from his notes. "Even in murder?"

"Even so. We just have to wait and see how it turns out. We may see it in this life, or maybe the next, but we will see it."

"I admire your belief," said Luke. "Most of us would find that hard to do." *Maybe He can explain how God allowed Kristy's passing some day*, he thought as he said, "If we can, let's start with Susan. She seems to have been very private. I know she attended UMO majoring in finance and quit her senior year. I assume from Carl's age she must have gotten pregnant and for whatever reason decided not to continue. Anything you can share to fill the gaps would be very helpful."

"Yes, Susan. She did not have it easy. She was a drug baby. Her mother overdosed when she was a teen and her father was never known. That put her in the system. Eventually she ended up in Skowhegan, living with some foster parents. I think they were in it for the money but they weren't abusive. She did well in school and was accepted to the University of Maine, but she was on her own. She got a couple scholarships, enrolled in a work–study program and funded the rest with student loans. She did very well. Straight A's. She dated like most college girls, but in her Junior year, she fell in love."

Luke looked at his notes. "That would be Mr. Lawrence King?"

"That sounds right. As you surmised, yes, she did get pregnant. That was the beginning of a downward spiral. Despite not knowing the Lord at that time in her life, she knew enough that if she was going to have a child, it had to be in a family setting. She wanted to break the cycle that she grew up in. I wouldn't call it a shotgun wedding, but she may have hinted about an abortion. He didn't want that. He was, she said, an honorable man and they both agreed to marry. I think they had known each other for only three months. The baby was due in the Spring."

Immediately Luke's eyes shifted from his notebook to the pastor. "Spring, you say?"

"Yes. I know why you are asking and I'm about to get there. She maintained her studies even as the pregnancy weighed her down. They were both excited. Mr. King was a senior about to graduate. They were going to have a son. He received several offers, some from some firms in big cities but he settled on an accounting firm in Bangor so she could complete her senior year and graduate. They thought they had things planned out, but God had another plan in mind."

Here we go again, thought the detective. "Another plan?" he asked.

"God has a way of switching tracks on our best laid plans and taking us somewhere else. She had a stillbirth. That was the first calamity. They were both devastated. She went into depression. She started to drink. That violated one of her cardinal rules after growing up the way she did. Susan couldn't fault her husband. She said he supported her and tried to console her as best he could, but the downward spiral had too much momentum."

"And this is God's plan?" asked Luke and immediately wishing to retract the question.

"Skepticism is a good quality, Luke," replied Joe unfazed. "Anyway, she heard from a friend in Skowhegan that her freshman roommate at Orono was also pregnant. This girl was going to spend the summer with her in Skowhegan to hide her pregnancy from her mother and then give it up for adoption. The baby was due during the Fall semester. Susan immediately thought that was the solution to fill the void from her miscarriage. She talked her husband into agreeing."

"How did that work out?" asked the detective.

"As you might expect. Not well. They adopted the boy. That's Carl. But it did little to assuage her depression. She continued to drink and mope. Her grades started to slip. She didn't look well. Mr. King, I guess, started to think about himself. He had more grandiose ideas than working for a small firm in Bangor for the rest of his life. The main reason he stayed with her was gone in his mind. He couldn't bring himself to view Carl as his own child. Anyway, you know the end. It was a short marriage."

"That must have crushed her given the state you just described."

"You would have thought," continued the reverend, "but like I say, God always has a plan. Yes, she sank deeper. There she was . . . with a baby . . . no husband . . . and no income. She had to quit school in her last semester. She got a job as a secretarial aid with some little company, but half of what she made went to child care. The downward spiral accelerated. Her drinking got worse."

The detective kept his face in his notebook with eyebrows raised.

"Patience, my dear boy," smiled the reverend patting the detective on the hand. "It gets worse. And that is how it gets better."

Worse? That's how it gets better? Am I the only one confused? The detective kept his nose down.

As if reading Luke's mind, Joe said, "Spiritual laws are contrary to earthly laws, Luke. The way up is always down."

Am I hear to investigate a murder or hear a sermon? Maybe both, he thought.

"She started to neglect Carl and that got the attention of a neighbor. This neighbor threatened to call child services. That's when she finally realized she could not make it on her own. The neighbor, not coincidentally I might add, was active in Alcoholics Anonymous. She took Susan to her first AA meeting. It was there she started recognize that there was a power greater than herself, a power she needed to conquer her demons."

"This is the good part, I assume," said Luke.

"You're getting it. Everyone needs to come to the conclusion that God is the only power in the universe and that only Jesus Christ has the answer. Like snowflakes, God never uses the same way twice."

Luke's poised hand had stopped taking notes. The old pastor paused as if waiting for an answer to an unasked question.

"Anything ringing a bell there, Luke? Ever feel like you were in the throes of hell and later look back just to see God was there all along?"

As if someone had conjured up some old snapshots and flashed them before Luke's face, he could see himself holding Kristy's hand during the last few moments of her life. There was a look on her face that he did not remember seeing then. It was a look of peace, a look that said, "it's OK—I'm OK."

"Uh . . . maybe," he said pulling himself out of his daze. *What's going on here?* he wondered. "OK . . . so, at this point she cleans herself up. And then she finds Kevin and Woodspring, I guess?"

Joe nodded with a shade more sad on his face. "She met him at an AA meeting. I'm not sure where. She may have still been on the rebound and he . . . well, he seemed to be what she needed at the time. He had his problems but he had a job and seemed to have his act together. He could be somewhat charming when he wanted to."

"I know the type."

Joe nodded again. "I met them when they came to Woodspring. That was his hometown. AA had given her the start but she knew she needed more than the generic God AA espoused. She found our little church and I watched her fall in love with God. She was baptized and so was he. They appeared to be starting out pretty well until he started to fall off the wagon. He couldn't hold a job for any length of time. She got a steady job at Morris Lumber as a bookkeeper and enjoyed it. It wasn't very good money, but she became the breadwinner. As time waned on, he just couldn't hold it together. He was jealous of being kept by a woman, though he never turned the money down. Things got more and more abusive. You know how these things go. She would show up with bruises, or a black eye, sometimes something worse. We visited him on one occasion and were stopped at the front door by the business end of a shotgun. Susan was not a weak woman like the ones typical of staying in an abusive relationship because they were scared or had no place to go. No. She was determined not to have another failed marriage. She thought that was what God wanted. She prayed for him. Nothing changed. Finally she recognized God had something else in mind. This wasn't going to work and for Carl's sake, she had to leave. Kevin was getting more abusive to him also. We knew he would try to stop or find her. I had contacts with a battered woman's shelter and made all the arrangements. Of course, by that time, I had left Woodspring and was communicating with her by phone. I had no idea she hadn't made it until someone called me and told me that Carl was still living at home. I knew that couldn't be right. I called the shelter and sure enough, she never showed up."

"What did you do then?"

"I called the Woodspring police station and was told they had no probable cause to investigate. You see, despite all the abuse, Susan never reported any of it. She had quit her job. Her car and belongings were gone. They had nothing on file to suggest she did anything other than leave."

The detective just nodded. "I know."

"So, I took a ride myself to check it out. I was met at the door again by Kevin and told in no uncertain terms to get off the property and never come back. He meant it. Then I went to talk to Pastor Huff. He and I discussed my concerns. He promised to keep an eye on Carl and let me know if there were any changes. I never heard anything more."

"Not surprised," said the detective taking a sip of coffee. "You have answered a lot of open questions. At some point, I need to share some of this with Carl. The only thing I can tell you is I am sure we will at least get justice for Susan. Thank you and thanks for the lunch."

"No problem, Luke. What about Carl? Tell me how he is doing. Who is taking care of him?"

"Actually, he has decided to take care of himself. He's sixteen now and has the means. But please don't worry. I have eyes on him. He has more maturity than most adults I know."

"That doesn't surprise me. Well, anything I can do. He's welcome to come here."

"I'll let him know."

The two of them rose and headed for the door. Luke slipped his shoes on and grabbed his coat.

"Oh . . . oh, I almost forgot," said Joe heading for the bookcase. "A copy of my book, *The Lost Coin*." He handed it to Luke.

"Thanks. I'll read it."

"Keep me informed of your investigation and don't hesitate to call me about anything."

"Uh . . . before I go, this is kind of off the subject, but you said something that sort of baffles me."

"What's that?" asked Joe.

"You said God had something else in mind for Susan when she decided to leave. You've mentioned God's plan a few times today. How could her being murdered be part of God's plan?" Luke stood as still as a statue as he waited for the answer.

The old pastor smiled. "I hate to give you a riddle, Luke. God uses everything for good, even evil. But you have to have eyes that see. Keep looking. And you will see." He shook Luke's hand.

Luke felt like the befuddled student whose answered question only served to confuse more. *That's it? And what about Kristy? How is that God's plan? That's all I need is one more riddle to contend with,* he thought as he worked his way out of the woods, one eye checking his cell phone for a signal. Finally he had a couple bars.

"Hi, Sarah . . . fine. How is everything there? . . . . . I got a lot of information. Confirming what your DNA results revealed, Susan was not the birth mother but neither was Lawrence King the supposed birth father. They adopted him from a single mother, a sophomore at the time at UMO. Let's check the adoption agencies in Orono and Bangor first. That is where Carl was born. . . . . Great. I'll be back in the office later."

XIX

CARL AND Kathy were giddy as they admired their new driver licenses.

"You should have seen the look on his face when he realized he was sitting in an unmarked police cruiser," Carl laughed. "No wonder they call it the Intimidator."

"I know," said Kathy. "And when you got out and I got in, he didn't know what to think. I think if I had accidentally turned on the siren his head would have hit the ceiling."

Luke chuckled as he walked into the kitchen shaking his head. "Oh, youth," he said.

"Tell me about it," said Eva checking the turkey in the oven. "Looks like a couple more hours. Are you going to tell him today?"

"Yes. He needs to know. I think we'll all sit down after dinner. I'm not sure what kind of a reaction we will get. He's grownup way more than his years, but it's a lot to swallow to find out that the person who you thought was your birth mother is not."

"What about Kathy? Should she be there?"

"I think so. The two of them seem to have connected in some . . . I don't know . . . way."

"You need me to spell it out for you?" said Eva with a wink.

"No . . . no. It's good. Kathy has known she was adopted from an early age. I think she will be a very soothing voice to however he takes the news. Someone he can relate to."

"You're a wise man," she said giving him a peck on the cheek. "But don't let it go to your head."

"Don't worry. I have plenty of checks and balances," he said with a mock growl. He peeked through the kitchen door. Kathy and Carl were sitting closer together on the couch talking faster than he could hear.

"Dad promised to take us, I mean you—I'm just along for the ride—car shopping tomorrow. So, what kind of car are you going to get? I know there isn't one in my near future. I'm so jealous." As soon as Kathy said it, her excited face fell ten stories. "I mean . . . I didn't mean it that way . . . jealous."

"It's OK, Kathy. I know what you meant," he said touching her hand. Like a mind meld, he sensed the same mixture of excitement and sadness in her as he felt, two things that should have been mutually exclusive but somehow were not. "So, what do you think I should do? I can't afford a new car."

Her face lit up again like a light bulb plugged into a high voltage outlet, but then dimmed to something more comfortable to the eyes. "I know what I'm thinking," she said. "That yellow Mustang convertible we passed this morning. However . . . Dad, who might as well be your Dad, as you will see," she continued with a knowing smile, "will try to make you get something more practical."

The thought of having a real dad suddenly snatched Carl into a make believe world he sometimes visited. But he was just a visitor. He had no real dad.

"Carl . . . Carl," said Kathy sliding her hand up and down in front of his face. "Earth to Carl."

"Uh . . . sorry," he said. "Yeah . . . I saw that Mustang. I think they installed a tractor beam on it. It pulled me pretty hard. But, I guess you're father is right. . ."

"Well, we can't say he is right. He hasn't said anything yet."

"We can pretty much assume," Carl laughed. "I think I know him that much. I need something practical. At least for now."

"Kathy, I need some help setting the table."

Kathy looked up to see Eva poking her head out from the kitchen. "Be right there."

Luke came out and turned on the TV. "What do you say? Let's see how the Cowboys–Redskins game is going."

"OK."

"What do you think of Eva's fizzy pear ginger punch?" asked Luke making a sour looking face.

Carl laughed. "Good."

"Good answer, son. And you better nibble some on of those little black penguins of Eva's . . . even if you don't like olives . . . and don't forget Kathy's deviled eggs," he said nudging Carl. "It may be true that the way to a man's heart is through his stomach, but the way to a woman's heart is by praising their cooking even if your stomach doesn't agree."

Luke enjoyed his joke alone. Carl just sat back feeling like a sojourner that had been too long out in the cold finally finding solace on the warm hearth of strangers.

By halftime, he and Luke were pulling out a bird so big that Carl couldn't believe it came out of that small oven. He remembered the small turkey he and his mother would share between them each Thanksgiving. His stepfather, who was often on a drunk anyway, always considered Thanksgiving as license to run off with his drinking buddies for a couple days.

Carl wondered where they would put it. The table was like a painted canvas with no place to add another dab of color. Mashed potatoes, sweet potatoes, stuffing, cranberry sauce, casseroles, homemade rolls, and a whole bunch of things Carl didn't recognize.

They managed to squeeze it next to Luke. Carl froze stiff in admiration like a well-trained pointer pup that had seen the mother of all fowl.

Luke laughed. "Sit down right there," he said, "across from Kathy."

Luke carved up the bird and sat down. "I guess maybe we'll say a prayer, and if anyone would like to share what they are thankful for, please feel free."

Luke gave thanks for what they were about to receive. It was a simple prayer. Then he thanked God for Eva, for Kathy, and for Carl. Eva thanked God for Luke, Kathy, and Carl. Kathy thanked God for Dad, Eva, and Carl.

With each prayer of thanksgiving, Carl was weighed down with more and more emotion until the bolts he had used to contain it could no longer stand the pressure.

"Thank you," he trembled unable to keep all his tears in check. "Thank you for letting me be a part of this family if only for a short time."

There was silence for a few moments as Kathy and Eva dabbed their eyes with napkins. Then there was the call, "Let's eat," from Luke and the silence was replaced with the clanking of passing dishes, utensils, and revived chatter.

Carl had forgotten about the homemade pumpkin pie. He may have miscalculated, but, nevertheless, it would not be denied. He slathered it with a thick layer of real whipped cream ignoring any resistance from his belly pressing against his belt. It was too good.

The four of them cleared off the table and retired to the living room with their coffees. At least two of them loosened their belts. They talked about school. Kathy wanted Carl to try out for the play that would perform around Christmas. Carl needed a little more convincing. They talked about Friday, what Carl wanted to talk about. The big shopping day for a car. Kathy would forego the Black Friday sales to go with them. Eva would not. Then the banter seemed to dwindle and Carl could feel the tone descend an octave. Then it got quiet.

Finally Luke said, "Carl, there are some other things we need to talk about. Some things we have uncovered in the investigation. Things you need to know."

"OK," he said putting down his coffee and sitting up straight. Eva and Kathy looked at each other.

"If you remember, we took samples from you to check your DNA against any other DNA we might find as evidence in the house."

Carl nodded.

"Well, when it came back, we found something unexpected. It did not match your mother's at all."

Carl stared at Luke. "What does that mean?" Then it dawned. "Are you saying that she isn't my mother?"

"Oh, she most certainly is your mother, Carl. Don't ever think anything else. But she is not your birth mother. And the man in the picture . . . you know . . . the one you showed me in your bedroom? He is not your birth father. They adopted you. When they divorced, she moved here and married Kevin."

Carl's face turned expressionless. His brain froze as if trying to process a question with no answer.

Luke broke the silence. "So, the next step is to try and find out who your biological parents are. We're working on that right now."

"What if I don't want to know," mumbled Carl staring at the floor.

"Maybe not," said Luke, "but someone out there might be the key to your future."

"Future," he said almost mocking. "It's just another one that didn't want me. That's pretty much how it goes."

Luke's face mirrored Carl's as if in a symbiotic relationship. "Maybe, Carl. Look I know how you feel."

"How's that?" he asked.

"Carl, my parents didn't want me. I was dumped into the system, passed around from foster home to foster home. No one even wanted to adopt me. I do know how you feel. But I worked it out. And from what little time I have known you, I know you will to."

Carl studied Luke's face as if seeing him for the first time.

"And I'm adopted, Carl," injected Kathy. "My biological parents put me up for adoption the day I was born. I don't even know who they were."

The tense lines in Carl's face softened as if his anger had been popped like a balloon. He looked over at Eva. "You too?"

Eva shook her head. "No. My mom raised me as a single mother. My dad left when I was small."

Everyone looked around the room at each other, speechless. Suddenly they jumped as Carl suddenly burst into an uncontrollable belly laugh. "So this is like some island of castaways."

Kathy was the first to catch the contagion. Then Eva and Luke joined in forming some unmelodious yet harmonious fugue. Tears streamed down their cheeks tapering off to a few sniffles until the only sound was the tic toc of a grandfather clock watching unamusedly in the corner with about as much personality as a cigar store Indian.

"More pie?" asked Eva poking Luke.

"Sounds like a good idea," he replied. Carl and Kathy seemed not to hear.

"Let's eat it in the kitchen," said Eva beckoning for Luke.

Kathy moved closer to Carl deep in thought. They stared at the walls together for several minutes. The clock maintained its indifference.

"Are you OK?" she finally asked taking his hand. He made no effort to withdraw it.

He looked deep into her blue eyes and saw nothing but trust. "Yeah. I am. Just confused. I'll figure it out."

"I know you will. For me, it wasn't so much of a shock. I was told as soon as I could understand what it meant. That made it kind of seamless. I never knew anything but the love of my father and mother. It didn't seem like it made any difference. I never thought it odd. As I get older, I do think more and wonder who they were, or are."

"Maybe if my mother had done the same thing, it would have been more natural. I don't know why she didn't tell me. And I don't understand how parents could give up their children in the first place. That doesn't make sense."

"That's certainly something I've thought about a lot. My mother passed me a lot secrets before she died that helped me understand."

Luke, who was feebly helping Eva with dishes strained at the kitchen door to hear.

"What are you doing? Eavesdropping?" she whispered.

"I'm a detective," he replied in a low voice. "She said something about Kristy's secrets."

Eva rolled her eyes.

"I'm supposed to keep my eyes open."

"For what?" she asked.

"I don't know. I was just told to keep looking by some old pastor who is either very sagacious or very looney. I'm not sure which."

"Give me that plate," she said mumbling to herself. "I'll do the dishes myself or they'll never get done."

Carl perked up. "Secrets? What kind of secrets?"

Kathy pulled a necklace out of her sweater. It was a gold heart shaped pendant with a cross embedded in the center. "Are you a Christian?"

"I thought I was," he replied. "I'm not so sure anymore."

"Well," she started as Luke strained to hear, "one of the things she taught me was Romans 8:28, *all things work together for good to those that love God.*"

"How is all this good? Your mother died of cancer. My biological mother abandoned me. My adopted mother was murdered. How can anyone find good in that?"

"I know. It doesn't make any sense, does it? Unless you know how God works. God is love. There is nothing that happens to us that doesn't happen because of love, because that is who He is. Even if it seems the opposite. I would never have known real love if it hadn't been for being adopted by my parents. I would never have known about faith and how love shines and conquers death had it not been for what my mother went through. No, I would never have known all this. Never known God the way I do. She gave me this to keep me reminded. The cross in the heart of God. To remind me that Christ conquered death through laying His life down for us. That even in death, we are more than victors. So you're right. It doesn't make sense to the uninitiated."

Carl listened intently. So did Luke.

"Even in murder?" asked Carl.

"In everything, Carl. He is there. Even in tragedy. You don't know how your life would have gone if you hadn't been adopted by her. You told me yourself. She saved your life. She drew him away long enough for you to escape. You don't know how it is going to go now. And look at your new extended family. What about us?"

Carl smiled.

"God has great plans for you. We just don't know what they are yet. We only know you are going to be a great writer. Who knows what impact you will have on people's lives?"

"How old are you?" asked Carl.

"The same as you, beyond our years," she laughed.

Their heads jerked toward the kitchen as Luke's cell phone pierced the silence and he almost fell through the swinging doors.

"I got it," he said red faced and went back into the kitchen.

"Hi, Sarah. What do you have? . . . that's OK, you aren't interrupting. I wanted to know as soon as possible . . . say that again . . . Les Enfants? . . . that was the adoption agency? . . . OK, then. Let's get the court order so we can open up the records and locate his biological parents. Thanks. And have a happy Thanksgiving. Sorry you had to pull the holiday detail."

Eva watched the color drain from Luke's face. "What is it?"

"Carl. He was adopted through Les Enfants in Bangor."

"So?"

"That is where we got Kathy," he replied in a vacant tone.

XX

IT IS said that justice is blind. Todd Everett, the county D.A., sat in his office staring at his statuette of Lady Justice all dressed up with her blindfold, scales, and sword as the Cook file was laid in front of him. The Woodspring home town boy made good, however, had a different idea. Justice needed to rip off the blindfold and see with its eyes. This guy was guilty. All the scales did was provide a spot for thumbs with nefarious motives to be placed.

He couldn't remember when the last time anyone had been prosecuted for capital murder in the quiet town of Woodspring. The only thing close was thirty five years ago and it was never prosecuted. The lukewarm investigation turned into a cold case. But Todd remembered the day Cyrus Watson, a thirteen year old paperboy and his friend, went missing. The suspect was always known, but justice peeked from under its blindfold just enough to see a boy from the wrong side of the tracks, white trash that carried no weight on the scale of justice. He remembered his criminal law professor telling him he had a chip on his shoulder. "So what if I do?" he countered. The professor looked at him as if seeing a passion he hadn't noticed before. "Then channel it to make a difference," he said and walked away.

Every so often he would check on the cold case of his lost friend. It just gathered another layer of dust. He hoped Luke Small, whom he had recommended to Chief Sullivan, would be able to add a new perspective to the case. But it would have to wait. Right now he was determined that Susan Cook would not be buried the same way in the cold case files.

"Sir, Detective Small is here," came the voice on the speaker phone.

"Thanks, June. Please send him in . . . and please bring us some coffee . . . lots of it . . . black."

Detective Small walked in with a half grin. "Might take a while, huh?"

"Maybe," the D.A. grimaced. "So, Luke, please have a seat. How are these backwoods treating you?"

Detective Small laughed. "Just fine. These are my kind of people."

"Bit more laid back than Boston, eh?"

"I would have thought, until the first case I walk into is all Déjà vu. Maybe not as much of a difference as you think."

"I hear you. Hopefully a little less quantity. I liked Boston OK. We had some interesting cases, didn't we? But I'm glad to be back in the sticks. And Kathy? How is she doing?"

"Very well. Very involved in school activities. Might even have a boyfriend."

"Oh, good. Guess I didn't steer you wrong bringing you up here then."

"No. We're doing well."

"And I understand even Dad might have a girlfriend," said Todd with a wink.

"Might," said Luke leaving the rest to imagination.

"It's about time," said Todd. "I'm glad for you. OK, down to business."

Todd's secretary came in with a pot of coffee and set it on his desk with two cups.

"So, our Chief couldn't make it over to our little shire town?"

"He seemed to think it would be better handled between the two of us. Without his input."

"Yeah, well there is a reason for that. I am sure you are aware of how Charley Wickes got his job in the first place."

"I've heard. His father is best friends with Peter."

"Right. He'll keep it at arm's length. Probably smart. Charley's reputation started long before he became a police officer. I was a senior when he was a freshman. He was a jock and all that, and pretty good, but he was a bully even then. He hasn't changed. Chief Sullivan has had to endure a few embarrassments due to Charley. If you were to see his personnel file, he's had more than a few complaints. All of which seem to get dropped before they go too far. That has been his MO all along. This will be the ultimate embarrassment and may cost Peter his job. If this goes to trial, Charley is implicated by association, an accessory after the fact at least or maybe even murder. Give me what we have so far."

"Well, we've pretty much hit a plateau. We have the frantic 9-1-1 call from Carl Cook that was abruptly cut off. He is the only witness to the events of that night and he did not actually see the fatality take place. He was beaten severely. We have the medical records for that. He apparently escaped the house before the officer who responded showed up. That, of course, was Charley Wickes. When he arrived on the scene, he testifies there were just the two of them having a routine domestic dispute. He broke it up and when he discovered it was because she wanted to leave, he made sure she was able to do that safely.

"There are several inconsistencies with Charley's story. His log shows him leaving at eleven that night, but he said he may have stuck around to console his buddy after she left because it was the end of his shift. Now he's changed his story. It was a long time ago, he said. Couldn't remember all the details. Now he says he just resolved the dispute and left at eleven. She was getting cleaned up in the bathroom when he left. Kevin Cook, of course, will corroborate whatever he says."

"He knows where this going. He's no fool, but the more they change the story, the deeper they will sink."

"Exactly. Carl is sure Wickes was there long after eleven, but he was only half conscious. The defense would beat him up on that. Her body being found so close to the residence works to support our case. Kevin will say she must have tried to return for something, maybe Carl, in the dead of night through the woods and that some accident must have befelled her. The defense will no doubt put that out there, but I doubt any juror would buy it. The fact that she left Carl is not believable either. We would have plenty of witnesses to support that."

"I agree. What about hard evidence?" asked Todd.

"It's all circumstantial. The residence was sterilized. We know there was blood there simply because Carl was bloodied before he crawled out the back door. Yet nothing was found. It was professionally cleaned by someone who knew how to get rid of evidence. And then there's the mythical bat. It's a collector's item signed by Ted Williams. Apparently Kevin was very fond of it. So fond of it that I haven't given up on the possibility that he may have kept it. I am sure that is the murder weapon. If we had that, that would seal the deal. But we don't. Then there is the missing vehicle. We are checking to see if it was sold in some other state. I haven't given up on that either, but so far nothing."

"I see," said Todd rubbing his chin. "Reasonable doubt. That, as you know, is what we have against us. I hate it when you know with everything in your body that the person is guilty, but there might be just enough to create the possibility of so-called reasonable doubt. Her quitting her job with the full intention of leaving that night along with arrangements made to receive her at a shelter . . . that doesn't help us. And we have the word of a police officer against a minor. I don't have to tell you we won't be able to use Charley's personnel history in court."

"I know," shrugged the detective. "We don't have any prior charges for abuse for Susan, but we do have plenty of evidence to prove that it did happen. Mrs. Cook was a Christian. She believed in forgiveness. I don't fault her for that, but she forgave one time too many. We do have Carl's testimony of physical and mental abuse and just the fact that she was heading for a battered women's shelter is de facto evidence she was abused. That definitely works in our favor."

"Is there anything about Susan Cook's life that might be dredged up by the defense?"

"Well, she had a history of drug and alcohol abuse, but that was years ago. She's a sponsor in AA and had been sober for at least fourteen years."

"Hmmm . . . they will want to use that but I'm sure we can get the judge to disallow it."

"It also turns out that Carl is not her biological son. She adopted him during a previous marriage that didn't last. I can't see where that plays into this case but we are running that down through the adoption agency."

"Probably not germane but see where it goes. Anything else?"

"A couple other things. She had a life insurance policy. They have a record of someone trying to find out if they could cash in the policy without a death certificate. No name was ever given, but the inquiry itself is still a bit of evidence in our favor. They have the call recorded. She also had a substantial savings account. She closed it out a couple days before she went missing. Her closing it out doesn't help us, but we found what probably remained of the money hidden in Kevin's bedroom. It was a week after she went missing when he showed up with a new pickup truck. More circumstantial evidence."

"True. We have a lot. We just don't have the final nail for the coffin. Like you said, if we could come up with the murder weapon, we could put this to bed. Or another witness to come forward. Is that possible?"

"One of the theories we are working on," said Luke, "is the possibility of additional collusion. If you think about all that had to be done before morning light . . . getting rid of the body . . . getting rid of the vehicle and belongings . . . sanitizing the place. That's a mouthful."

"You could be right. Let's not give up on that. What about Officer Wickes. What is he doing while this investigation is going on?"

"He's keeping quiet for the most part. He has been messing around in the evidence room, but there isn't anything there that will help him. All the evidence will come out before the trial. My sources tell me he is in contact with Kevin Cook, I'm sure to keep their evolving story straight. They meet at some sleazy bar out in the woods."

"Barb's Deepwoods Saloon?"

"Yeah. How did you know?"

"I know where all the skeletons are in that town. A place of ill repute would be a generous review for that establishment. Well, given what we have, we could go for it. We have a pretty good chance of winning. It's just I hate *pretty good* chances. When you're ninety percent in, you're ten percent out. The question is, do we roll the dice given those odds? What do you say?"

Their faces went through several iterations as they pondered the decision until they finally synchronized.

"Book him!"

XXI

WHAT A difference a day makes. The indifferent color of gray turned to green with chameleonic agility. Those who before had no problem ignoring the pitiful orphan boy now stood open mouthed as he rolled into Woodspring High School in a new Honda CR–V and Kathy Small on his arm. A long drive to Freeport over the weekend added the finishing touches—a flashy red fleece lined LL Bean jacket, black leather gloves, and the trademark boots, insulated this time. And she made him get a haircut. Kathy was pleased with her handiwork. They walked to their lockers no differently than before, but somehow it was as if they had stepped out of a wormhole and become magically visible.

"Who's the new kid," whispered one student as they fumbled in their lockers.

"Beats me . . . wait . . . I think that's Carl Cook."

"You're kidding. The murderer's kid? Just who does he think he is?" jabbed Bobby Martin, the captain of the Woodchucks basketball team.

"How did someone like him get her?" chimed in one of his groupies.

"White trash," snickered another. "Both of them. That's how."

"I can't believe she's on the cheerleading squad," said Judy Wickes, Bobby's girlfriend.

Carl had never felt the color of green and for sure never expected to be on the other side of it. If he finally had something, it was a far price to pay. He waded through the thick buzz. Peering eyes quickly shied away as he passed.

Principal Thompson's rotund body appeared around the corner. His eyes locked on Carl as he bee lined in his direction. "How are you doing, Carl?" he asked as if the building were void of any other occupants.

"Uh . . . fine, sir," Carl replied.

"Good. You let me know if you need anything." He patted Carl on the shoulder and continued his rounds as everyone wondered what made him so special.

Carl looked over at Kathy who mirrored the same question mark on her face. All this dichotomic attention was a new experience. He had not changed. But something had. Maybe it was his imagination, but the teachers looked at him differently. It was if they were performing a visual physical exam each time he passed by. It was creepy. He knew why. He had heard them complaining about having to take training on their own time, Mandatory Reporting of Abuse and Neglect.

They grabbed their books and marched toward their journalism class ignoring the stares as if for once they were the only humans on the planet. Kathy had moved to be beside Carl. Mr. McKinley was doing his usual thing on the black board. As the room filled up, the noise got proportionally louder until Mr. McKinley rapped a ruler on the desk. The Catholics shut up immediately.

Carl had noticed a change in his teacher as well, but in a positive way. His teaching had really improved. He was less intense, more patient, less lecturing and more coaching. He had taken more interest in his students.

As the bell rang, Mr. McKinley beckoned for Carl to come down front. Kathy waited in the hall. "Carl, if you have a few minutes at the end of the day, I would like to talk to you about your writing."

"Yes, sir," he replied. "I'll be staying late anyway. I'm going to try out for the play. And then we have the game tonight."

"Good for you, Carl." He could see Mr. McKinley's eyes light up. "I'm glad to see you getting involved. I'll see you here around . . . say three thirtyish."

"What's that all about?" asked Kathy as they headed for Mr. Bates algebra class.

"I don't know. He just said he wanted to talk about my writing after school. Maybe I need some remedial work."

"Don't be crazy," she said poking him in the arm. "He probably wants to tell you what a genius you are."

"Right."

Mr. Bates had changed also, but more subtle like he wasn't so certain of himself. His manner was softer, more attentive to his students. That, however, did not make it any easier to figure out what X was.

"Some genius," he whispered to Kathy. "I'm a writer, not a mathematician."

She rolled her eyes. "Don't worry. I'll get you through it."

"Right. You're going to be the engineer. I forgot."

They ducked into their book as Mr. Bates turned to see who was talking.

At the end of class, Mr. Bates said, "Carl . . . just a second please."

Carl walked down front as the classroom drained out. *Guess I'm going to get it for talking,* he thought, *or tell me I'm wasting my time. Drop the class. He won't have to ask twice.*

"Carl, I just wanted to let you know that Pastor Huff is gone and that Pastor Theriault is going to be back this Sunday. I just thought you might like to know that. I think there will be a lot of changes for the better. Maybe give it another chance?"

"Thank you, sir," Carl said. "Maybe."

The deacon didn't press it any further.

At lunchtime, Carl met up with Kathy and Andy in the cafeteria line.

"Looks like you're filling out," said Andy as Carl heaped his plate.

Carl looked over at Kathy. "Well, someone is making sure I eat better. And of course, those fried Spam sandwiches at Jumbo's didn't hurt."

Immediately visions of fried Spam sandwiches started dancing in Andy's head.

"Over here, Andy," said Carl poking him and pointing to their reserved place.

"So," said Andy stuffing his first chicken nugget in his mouth, "what part are you going to try out for?"

"I don't know. Maybe Julius Caesar," he replied. "He dies early on. What about you?"

"I think I'm going to work behind the scenes. On the set. No one needs to see this on the silver screen," he replied sucking in his stomach.

"Oh, don't sell yourself short," said Kathy. "Uh . . . I mean don't shortchange yourself. Uh . . . you know what I mean."

Andy laughed. "Right. Say, did you hear about Janet Collins?"

"No," said Carl. "What about her?"

"I guess the attention on abuse is working. Apparently she was being abused by her father. They say after seeing the courage you were showing, she finally had the nerve to confide it to Mrs. Beckett who reported it."

"Seriously?" Carl replied. "You know, that doesn't surprise me. I could see it in her eyes. It's like we know each other. And that entire family went to our church."

"Maybe that's why no one suspected," said Kathy, "but professing to be a Christian and being one have little to do with church."

"Well, things might change there too. That's what Mr. Bates wanted to tell me. Huff is gone and our old pastor is coming back. That's a real good thing. He really took an interest in the people."

"That was his way of apologizing. We'll go this Sunday," Kathy said, clearly more of a behest than a recommendation.

"We will," he said. "We will."

They slowly finished their lunch as Carl mulled over all the strange things he was witnessing and Andy continued to fantasize about those fried Spam sandwiches.

§§§

"Carl, there are a couple things I wanted to discuss with you. Do you remember that writing exercise you turned in a few weeks ago?" asked Mr. McKinley.

Carl could feel the emotion return to the pit of his stomach. "Yes. I'm not sure it deserved an A plus, though."

"It was a little dark," replied the teacher, "but it definitely deserved at least that."

A "little" dark? thought Carl wishing he could hide.

"That piece came directly from the heart. You, know you have a gift. That is how great writers are made . . . they risk it all. They paint pictures with words drawn from their own well of raw emotions and beliefs. You know, I had that passion once. But somewhere along the line I ran out of flint or something. I just couldn't make it spark. You're different. We all have different callings. What I have come to discover about myself is that my real passion is teaching."

Carl just stared at his teacher as if an alien had flown in from outer space and taken over his body. Why is he sharing all this personal stuff? he wondered.

"I see a lot of me in you at sixteen. I didn't have a mentor, though. No one to help me navigate, to point me in the right directions, to get the best education, to get the best chance to succeed. Don't get me wrong. I was bitter for a long time. But recently, with a little help from . . . well, let's say from this world and maybe another, I have come to realize that I am exactly where I am supposed to be doing what I am supposed to be doing. You do want to be a writer, correct?"

"Ye . . . yes, sir." he replied.

"Well, the schools with the best creative writing programs are hard to get in. And they aren't cheap. University of Virginia, Boston University, even Princeton. So I am going to make a deal with you. Number one, it won't be good enough just to ace this class. You have to ace them all and blow them away on the SAT's. I've talked to some of your teachers. They tell me you have all this in you and that you probably are dragging more unused talent behind you then anyone in the school. Do you understand?"

"Yes, sir."

"I know you do. So you and I are going to work extra hours on your writing. Get you in shape for the big day. These schools will require a masterpiece of a manuscript before they even look at your grades or SAT's. Are you good with that?"

"Yes, sir."

"And you are going to bear down on all your classes. Even Mr. Bates algebra. Correct?"

"Yes, sir."

"OK, enough yes, sirs" he said breaking the tension. He held out his hand. "Shake on it?"

"Uh . . . yes . . ." he nodded the affirmative and took his hand.

"Wait. The second thing, Carl. I want to apologize for not doing more to help you before. I knew you weren't exactly . . . being . . . let's say forthright about your injuries. We all knew. It was just easier to take what you said and go on. I was as guilty as anyone. I hope you can forgive me."

"Yes, sir. I do."

At that Carl turned and walked out wondering if maybe aliens had taken over the whole planet.

§§§

Men at some time are masters of their fates. The fault, dear Brutus, is not in our stars, but in ourselves, that we are underlings.

Carl wondered if Bobby Martin knew that when despite having an open man under the basket, he fired away the prettiest jump shot ever seen only to bounce rudely off the rim. Before the rebound could be snatched, the buzzer sent that electrifying reality check to each player that it was over. Like Pavlov's dogs, they went limp at the sound. Woodspring Woodchucks seventy eight. Jackman Tigers seventy nine. Bobby had thirty five of the Woodchuck points. He was great, just not great enough.

Carl hadn't paid much attention to the game with Kathy cheering in front of him, but he was glad he caught that last act. The script of Julius Caesar lay beside him. He couldn't believe Mrs. Slip gave him the part he wanted—Julius Caesar. But there weren't many jocks competing for the parts. Kathy drew Portia and Andy got the part of Brutus but was already worrying about stabbing Carl in the back. "Don't worry," he told Andy. "I'm used to it."

After the token good loser—good winner high fives, the girls and the boys headed for the locker rooms. He picked up the script and started reading it again as he waited for Kathy to reappear.

Most of the gym had cleared out. He could see David McKinley and Howard Bates lingering in a corner talking. *Now I know the world is coming to an end*, he thought. Mary was standing beside them. No one had seen her in quite a while. She was just now getting out of the house and socializing.

Carl stared at them a while and wondered if they were talking about him given both had called him aside that day. He shyly put his head back into the script when he saw Mary looking his way. When he looked up she was still studying him.

"Who is that boy?" asked Mary interrupting David and Howard.

"Who?" asked David.

"The boy in the bleachers. Reading."

"Oh, that's Carl Cook. The one I was telling you about. Remember. You read that piece he had written."

"Oh, yes. That poor boy." She kept staring.

"What is it?" asked David.

"I . . . I don't know. There is just something about him. I can't explain it. I can see why you want to help him."

The three of them moved toward the exit. Carl watched them out of the side of his eye. Mary's head kept turning back until she disappeared out of sight.

Then Kathy appeared, her usual smile hidden somewhere.

"Hey. How did it go?"

"I don't know. Girls can be catty. Seems like they're in heat or something." She turned red. "I mean . . . you know what I mean."

Carl laughed. "I do."

"That Judy Wickes. She's been repeating lies from her uncle why we left Boston. We moved here because my mother was from Bangor. Dad always wanted to move her back. We were just a little late."

"Everyone knows Officer Wickes. I wouldn't worry about it. Let's go."

Most of the cars were gone by the time they made it to the parking lot, just a few parents and teachers and the players who had cars. Carl brushed a soft layer of powder off the windshield. "I'll get this thing warmed up," he said.

They sat there for a few minutes to let the defroster do its thing. Kathy could just start to feel some warmth come though the vents as Carl strained to look at a dark vehicle parked in the farthest corner of the lot. It might have gone as empty, but Carl could see the telltale exhaust plume curling up around the lamppost.

"What is it?" she asked.

"Nothing," he replied as he put it in gear. "Thought I had seen that truck somewhere."

They pulled out on the highway toward Kathy's house.

The truck's headlights came on and started to follow.

XXII

LOVE'S FIRST kiss. Whether or not that did it, the Frog Prince was transformed into a handsome young man in a well-fitting dark suit sitting alongside Kathy in the front pew. As *Beulah Land* was softly sung on the platform, Luke Small had many questions bumping into each other, not the least of which was what was happening in front of him. The two of them had been coming in late every night after play rehearsals. There was never a concern of anything other than that going on. It was the thought of her being hurt, a pressure building in his heart that seemed to intensify each time he watched them together. She hadn't been so happy since they left Boston.

Luke dredged up her adoption papers from Les Enfants. The birth mother had been redacted on the original birth certificate. He would have to wait for Sarah to call with the court order to find out about Carl. *What was taking so long?* But he knew how the wheels of the legal system turned. It was as if they operated in a slow orbit detached from life on earth. He never liked it.

Their birthdays are a day apart, he reminded himself. But the time of birth on her certificate would not stop gnawing at him. Just a few minutes after midnight separated them. *It couldn't be*, he kept telling himself as if repeating it over and over would make it true. *She can't be his twin sister. They don't even look alike.*

Eva gave him a nudge. Startled, he looked around as if having forgotten where he was or how he got there. The little church was filling to capacity.

"Wow," she said. "For someone who was supposed to be something of a loner, I've never seen such a turnout."

Cars continued to roll in. There were several church parishioners he recognized from last Sunday's service he was dragged to by Kathy. David and Mary McKinley sat directly behind him. A couple other teachers he had seen during his interviews at Woodspring High School were there. Most he had never seen before. *There's a whole lot more to Susan Cook than anyone realized, Detective. Wake up. Detect.*

There were few pictures of Susan displayed, but barely enough room to move around for the flowers and cards. The tempo suddenly picked up as Howard Bates led the congregation in singing *I'll Fly Away*. He wasn't bad. Then the room hushed as the lanky old pastor took the podium.

"Welcome," he said, "back to Woodspring Baptist Church." He stopped and gazed around the sanctuary. "I'm Joe Theriault, the pastor here, and I have known Susan Cook a long time. It may seem like there are many unfamiliar faces in the pews this morning. They may think they are strangers but they are not. They all have one thing in common. They have all experienced the love of Christ through the human form of the person called Susan Cook."

The human form of Susan Cook? What does that mean? This guy is so different," thought Luke.

"Susan was not one for many words. She didn't believe in waste. She was not one to seek praise or the spotlight. She was praise personified. There are many verses I could use to describe her. But mostly, she would be like one of the elders in Revelation that cast their crowns before the throne and that would be a sufficient reward. She is the one who always thought more highly of others than herself, the one who was meek and lowly in heart, the one who served others, the one who poured out her life for others, even unto death. Make no mistake. Hers was a life fully lived. Many will ask how can that be so? Her life was cut short." He waved his hand around the room. "Well, let's see. You don't need another sermon on how she is in a better place. That's true, but we need to know how she made this a better place. How she changed lives. Real truth that has been experienced."

That was all he said. And then they started to come up, one after another, as if choreographed by some phantom director.

"Hello. My name is Helen and I am an alcoholic . . ." and she went on to tell how Susan had pulled her out of the depths of hell, how she had brought her to a saving knowledge of Jesus Christ, how her life was richer for having known her.

"My name is Jim. I was a drug addict. Susan found me overdosed in an alley. Little Susan somehow stuffed me in her car and took me to the hospital. But that isn't where she stopped. If she had, I would have been discharged and gone back to drugs. She shared her faith. About this man called Jesus Christ. This God man. I wouldn't have believed it if her eyes hadn't convinced me."

"My name is Joyce. I was in an abusive relationship. Susan prayed with me. She came to my aid when I needed it. She had no fear. We shared our personal experiences. She was the one who finally got me to realize I had to leave. It was just . . . just before she also decided it was enough for her also." Joyce could barely finish through the tears. "But it was too late for her. I should have been there for her . . ." She couldn't finish.

They kept coming in a never ending line, one after another. Yet no one attempted to leave. They wanted more. They sat upright and fixated on each story as the Christ became real to them through Susan Cook. Muffled tears could be heard between testimonials.

Finally, the last one stepped down. All eyes turned to Carl Cook as he slowly made his way to the podium and pulled out a sheet of paper with what he wanted to say. The sanctuary was ghostly quiet. As he looked out over the crowd he seemed to be unaware that they were waiting for him to speak. It was as if he was waiting for something. Then he took the sheet of paper and put it back in his jacket pocket.

"Hello," he said with a confidence beyond his years. "My name is Carl Cook. I am my mother's son. I was adopted. That is something I only recently found out. I've spent a lot of time over the last year feeling sorry for myself. I knew my mother didn't abandon me. I knew that in my heart. Yet I chose to believe that over the alternative which is the reason we are here today. Now I have learned that she took me when no one else wanted me. As I listen to all the lives touched by my mother, I am ashamed. It isn't that I was unaware of things she had done. It's just that until this day, I never appreciated her as I do now. I thought it was all about me. Selfish. But it wasn't. I was just one of many, many touched by her life. But I was the one that she gave her very life to save. I've heard a lot lately that somehow God has a plan for all of us, that He is everywhere in every situation. Even in death. The pastor said she lived a full life. Complete. I still don't totally understand that, but somehow I have been given something to believe in, thanks to all of you. I have never felt so humble. Thank you."

"Where did this boy get such wisdom?" Luke said to Eva looking straight ahead. She was less shy about the tears as she dabbed a few with his handkerchief. "I have never heard anything like that in my life."

The pastor stepped up and patted Carl on the back. "Carl, let me sum up what you just said with some of her favorite scriptures. From Isaiah," he said as he turned to the book.

Sing, barren woman, you who never bore a child; burst into song, shout for joy, you who were never in labor; because more are the children of the desolate woman than of her who has a husband," says the LORD.

"And from Psalm 127," he continued.

Like arrows in the hand of a warrior are the children of one's youth. Blessed is the man who fills his quiver with them!

"Carl," said the pastor, "when I look out over this congregation, I see nothing but arrows. Arrows that came from your mother's own bow. Her quiver was full. Her life well lived. Crowns that she will lay at the feet of the Lord Jesus Christ. Arrows that will fill many other quivers to proclaim His love."

"I was one of those arrows," Carl said as his eyes glassed over. "Just one of so many."

Pastor Theriault closed the Bible and gave Carl a hug. As Carl returned to his seat, *It is Well With My Soul* started to play in the background. Kathy's eyes couldn't wait to hug him. They sang one more song as people poured down the aisles and kneeled in front of the alter.

As each came up from the alter, they hugged Carl and said words of encouragement in his ear, men and women. Luke was overwhelmed with the outpouring. One woman made her way to the front and hugged Carl. "I have seen this woman somewhere," said Luke to Eva.

"You've seen everyone, Detective," she whispered back.

Luke looked at her. "I do have my head full of faces," he admitted. "I just can't remember how I know her."

Then he heard David McKinley say behind him, "I can't believe it. What is she doing her?"

Luke looked around and saw David having a similar Déjà vu reaction.

"Who is it?" asked Mary.

"I am almost sure that is my sister's college roommate at Orono."

"Maybe you should go talk to her," said Mary.

"There's a bit of a history there," David said rubbing her back. "I am pretty sure she doesn't want to talk to me."

Luke couldn't hear what the woman whispered in Carl's ear, but Carl's reaction grabbed his attention. As she walked off, Carl made an impulsive motion to follow her as others were still lined up to express their condolences. Kathy saved him by gently grabbing his elbow.

What was that about? thought the detective as he traced her movements to the exit. Just as she disappeared from sight he remembered. "The photograph!" he exclaimed quietly.

"What?" asked Eva.

"Excuse me," he said as he slipped by her to the aisle and started working his way to the back through the dense crowd. "Excuse me . . . sorry . . . excuse me . . .," but it was too late. He saw her get in a red Buick and drive off. *Oh no*, he thought kicking himself, *I lost her. Some detective. I may have just missed a big clue.* Then he remembered David's comments. *Maybe all is not lost.*

He returned to Eva. David and Mary were waiting in line to offer their condolences to Carl. He waited impatiently. David said the normal things. Mary said nothing. She just hugged Carl as if finding a long lost son. Finally they moved to let the next person step in.

"What is it, Mary?' David asked. "You seem awful taken with the boy."

"I don't know," she replied. "It's just . . . something. I can't explain."

Luke walked up and interrupted them. "Mr. McKinley," he said. "Could I have a word?"

David looked puzzled. "Certainly."

"That woman," he said.

"What woman?"

"The one I heard you say you knew. I have seen her in a photograph at Carl's house. Who is she?"

"Yes. I am pretty sure that was my sister's roommate in college. She's from Skowhegan, at least she was."

"Skowhegan? What is her name?"

"I remember her first name. Elizabeth. They called her Lizzy. I am at a loss on the last name. It will come to me."

"What was your sister's name?"

"Deborah," he replied. "What does that have to do with anything?"

"I'm not sure, David. I'm just trying to put some pieces of a puzzle together. I wasn't eavesdropping, but I did hear you say that she wouldn't probably want to talk to you. Is that something you would be willing to share?"

David thought for a second. "I'm not sure why you would be interested in that."

The detective made no effort to let it go.

"Are you going to the wake?" asked David.

"We are," he replied.

"We can talk there. Maybe I'll remember her last name by then."

XXIII

WOODSPRING WAS no different from many small towns. The house on the hill standing watch over the town usually belonged to some captain of industry to whom all owed subservience. Such was not the case with Dick Morris. The large two story log cabin home with the huge wrap around porch was a monument, yes, but its greatness was a humble monument in honor of the three generations of Morris's that had preceded him. His great grandfather emigrated from Ireland to become a lumber jack eking out an unforgiving living in tarpaper logging camps. Through hard work, they began as a one saw sawmill, each building on the other and now Morris lumber produced some of the most exquisite knotty pine paneling in the country. The fruit of his labor was on display throughout the house along with hardwood floors, hand hewn beams, and a stone fireplace large enough to roast a moose. This house was an open and warm invitation to any who would partake. And today many would.

Every flat space was laden down with some kind of refreshment or delicacy, as lavish as Woodspring was capable of offering. No expense was spared. Mourners rolled in filling the circular driveway with the overflow lining the road. No knocking would be tolerated. Walk on in.

Andy's bib was replaced with an apron as he was pressed into service along with his father and mother, hosts that personified grace. People distributed themselves through the ample rooms and the glassed in porch overlooking the valley below on the backside of the house. Chatter was immediate and spontaneous. Each wanted to hear each other's stories of Susan Cook.

Luke and Eva had waited for the church to empty and were the last to arrive with Carl and Kathy. From the bottom of the hill they were no less awed by the attendance.

"It looks like they all came," commented Eva.

As they walked up the driveway, the detective saw what he was looking for, the red Buick. *All is not lost*, he thought.

"Carl," Luke said, "that woman, the one toward the end . . . she whispered something to you that seemed to startle you. You almost ran after her. What did she say?"

"It was strange. She commented on how I had grown up to be such a fine young man as if she knew me."

"Do you know her?"

"I don't think so. Even stranger, she said she needed to talk to me. That's when I almost started after her."

"Remember that picture of you and your mother and dad? And the other woman in the picture?"

The bulb started to glow "Oh, yeah," he said as. "You're right. I wonder what she wanted to tell me."

"Well, you're going to find out. That's her car right there," he said pointing.

"Ever the detective," said Eva slightly shaking her head. "Just remember. This is a wake."

The detective paid no heed as he searched each room until he found her. She was talking to David and Mary McKinley in a corner by themselves. *I thought he didn't want to talk to her,* thought the detective.

As soon as she spotted Carl she immediately headed toward them. "Carl, I am so glad to finally meet you," she said giving him another hug.

"Do we know each other?" asked Carl.

"No. But I know your mother. Both your mothers."

Carl, Kathy, Luke, and Eva stood there with their mouths open like there was something they had missed.

"I'm sorry," she said. "I thought you knew."

David walked up behind her and said, "We need to sit down and talk. Privately."

§§§

Dick Morris opened the door to his ornate study furnished with two facing black leather couches, two matching easy chairs, a smaller stone fireplace complete with requisite bear skin rug, and a maple desk with hand carved legs and trim. The opulence was wasted on the seven person entourage whose anxious minds only focused on the woman in the photo.

Carl was already full from the emotional events of the day and the new drama about to unfold was like handing a drowning man a glass of water. *Did I hear her right?* he questioned himself. *Did she say I know both your mothers?*

They split into two groups as if knowing the seating assignments. David, Mary, and the woman in the red Buick sat across from Luke, Eva, Carl, and Kathy. The silence pierced the air as each fumbled for an ice breaker.

Finally David spoke up. "Let me start. This is Elizabeth Mills. I knew her as Lizzy in college. She was my sister's roommate at the University of Maine." David looked over at her and nodded. "More than a roommate. Her best friend. My sister was a freshman there when I was a senior. I was very close to her, very protective. I thought she needed me to look after her. You see . . . she and I came out of . . . well, let's say, a less than worldly environment. I was concerned that she could be taken advantage of. My fears were realized when in the Spring term she got pregnant. We discussed options. I tried to help her. I didn't such a good job."

David looked over at Lizzy. "I'm sorry, Liz. You were right. I was wrong."

Liz gave a nonjudgmental nod.

Mary's eyes stayed glued to Carl as David's eyes darted back and forth between Carl and Lizzy as he spoke.

Carl sat on the edge of his seat as if he was ready to blast off at any time. "What was her name?" asked Carl.

"Deborah, Carl. Deborah," said David. "Anyway, I'll let Liz tell you what happened after that. She stepped in and took care of Deb at a time when some of us, well . . . failed."

"Debbie," said Liz, "you have to remember was only nineteen years old. She had a very strict upbringing. The church she grew up in had left an indelible mark on her. She and I had many discussions about her experiences. There wasn't much that wasn't sin. When she got pregnant, she really thought she had committed the unpardonable sin, an abomination, anathema."

"It was very legalistic," interjected David, his face tensing up with memories, "to say the least. It would make Quakers look like a bunch of liberals play acting as Christians. The venal and mortal sins of Catholics were only a short list of everything that would send you to hell. She took it very seriously."

"When this happened," continued Liz, "she was beside herself. She didn't dare tell her mother. She considered some dark options. She even considered . . . well . . . we don't need to discuss that. We were able to talk her down. Everything she did was out of love. She thought the boy she loved . . . well, would stand by her. He didn't. He left. She was left to deal with it on her own. She was just a confused mass of jelly. But she was a very strong lady, determined to carry the weight of it by herself if that was the way it was. And she did. She did what she thought was best for the children.

"Her decision was to take you to term and put you out for adoption. She came to live with me that summer to keep it secret from her mother. Really everybody. We worked through an adoption agency in Bangor. But before they found someone that would adopt, Susan, your mother and friend of mine, had a miscarriage. She was devastated. The doctor told her she couldn't have any more children after that. When she found out about Debbie, she asked if she could adopt you. They hit it off. Debbie felt so good knowing you would be well taken care of by a loving family. Unfortunately for Susan, some of her reasons were flawed. She hoped that adopting you would save her marriage. It didn't. Nevertheless, she loved you as if she had borne you herself. I think you know that, don't you?"

"Yes."

"I lost track of Susan after her divorce. She seemed to go off the grid. No social media. Nothing. It wasn't until I saw her obituary in the Skowhegan paper that I realized it was she. I had to come."

"What about my birth mother and father? Where are they now?" asked Carl.

"Carl, I don't know where your birth father is. His name was Bob Castello. He went to work as an engineer somewhere in California."

"What about my birth mother? Where is she?"

David got real quiet and put his hand on Carl's shoulder. "Your mother, Carl," said David, his voice starting to choke up, "my sister, she died in a car accident. Just over a month ago."

Carl's eyes glassed over. Why he didn't know. He never knew this woman. "Two mothers in two years" he sighed to himself. "God's plan?"

"There's more, Carl," said Liz. She looked over at David. "I don't think David even knows this. You weren't the only one. She had twins. You have a sister. It was a surprise. I guess when you're getting charity care, they either neglect to tell you or they just aren't very thorough."

"A sister?" asked Carl his voice cracking and now unable to stop a tear. "I have a sister? Where is she?"

Liz grimaced. "I don't know, Carl. It was unexpected. Deborah didn't know she was carrying twins. The clinic never said anything. She was turned over to the same adoption agency in Bangor, the one that did the transaction for Susan."

"Les Enfants?" asked Luke.

"Yes. How did you know?" replied Liz looking at him like who is this guy?

Carl had the same look. *How would he know that?*

"Anyway, I don't think it took long to place her, but I wasn't involved. I'm not sure your mother even knew. I'm not sure she wanted to know at that time. She was so upset she couldn't think."

"Did she look for us?" asked Carl. Kathy reached over and took his hand.

"Carl, I think once she made her decision, she did her best not to look back. Not because she didn't love you. No, that wouldn't be true. It is because she loved you with all her heart. She believed that she had put you in the best family situation and was determined not to interfere with it. Her heart was broken. I know she wanted to find you, but she was a woman of conviction. She felt any contact would ruin the relationship you would have with your family. It was pure discipline on her part that made her able to stay away. She loved you and wanted the best for you. She never even told her husband. She walked it all alone. A very lonely road."

"But I do have family," he said in a confused statement.

"More than you know, Carl," said Liz smiling. "I know this is a lot all at one time, but you have another sister and a brother. Deborah had another set of twins after marrying a wonderful man. It's unbelievable, I know. They live in Florida."

"I guess they don't want to know me," said Carl.

"No, Carl. They most certainly do want to know you."

"Do you have a contact?" asked Luke switching to detective mode.

"I do. His name is Perry Richardson. He didn't know about you or your sister. I saw him at your mother's funeral. He is working right now to find you. I'll be calling him this afternoon to tell him the good news. You will find him one of the nicest persons you ever met. Now we just have to find your sister."

Carl looked over at David and Mary, exhausted. "So, I guess that makes you my uncle?"

David nodded with a sheepish smile. Mary's face had happier ideas in mind.

"What about my sister?" asked Carl to Luke.

"Don't worry, Carl," he replied patting him on the shoulder and eyeing Kathy, "we'll find her. I'm going to check right now with Sarah on the status of our court order."

Luke stepped out of the room as a more subdued conversation began. Carl couldn't get the questions out fast enough about his birth mother and how she knew Susan. Kathy just listened as all the secrets of Carl's life unfolded.

§§§

"Sarah, how are you? . . . Fine. We just came from the memorial service. Where do we stand on that court order for Les Enfants? . . . We just got it? Great . . . What's that? They said we were the third inquiry into this adoption? . . . Who else would be interested? . . . Privileged information, eh? . . . We'll have to make a trip to Bangor. You won't believe, though, we have a lot of information about Carl. I have some contacts. I'll fill you in when I get back to the office. And what about that hair sample of Kathy's? Did the DNA results come back? . . . OK, please give them a call and see if you can expedite it. Thanks. I'll talk to you later."

XXIV

BARBARA KEPT the mediator hid under the counter as another of her patrons was hauled out of the Deepwoods Saloon. It was nothing unusual. She often joked that she was a half-way house for those headed in the wrong direction on a one way street. In the end, it helped cut her losses. It was usually just one more tab that was never going to be paid anyway.

Kevin Cook, on the other hand, tried a resistance of sorts as his spaghetti arms flailed into the atmosphere only to have his head hit the oak floor with a resounding thud. They cuffed his drunken body. The last she saw of him was his boots dragged out the door.

Jerry Moss sat in the county jail waiting for his client to be presented. Normally he would shy away from Public Defender jobs, but this one might be newsworthy enough to jack up his reputation. Granted, it was a small map, but a good murder case might at least get him a noticeable pin on it. One thing for sure, his staple of DUIs and domestic abuse cases wasn't advancing him anywhere. He needed to be taken more seriously.

He nervously checked his watch. *What's the holdup?* He pulled out the discovery file one more time as he waited. The charge was murder, one of only two choices available. *That's a lot of circumstantial evidence,* he thought. *No charges of abuse until recently with the boy, but too much smoke there. Still, a lot points to her just leaving. There was a definite intent. They have a good case, but it has some soft spots. They know that. I'll bet worst case is we negotiate to manslaughter. They don't know whether or not it was done with malice, the key difference between murder and manslaughter, and they don't want to lose this case. District Attorney Everett already threw it out there but said we'd have to move on it before all the expense of trial preparation. I'll have to listen to all the righteous indignation, I suppose, but this guy is guilty of something. He'd be smart to go for the offer. But they never are.*

Still, he had to mentally start preparing a defense strategy just in case it were to go to trial. Forget about celebrity trials that go on for months. These backwoods trials go so fast that you blink and the defendant is either swinging from a tree or swinging at a victory party. You had to make an impact on the jury and you had to do it quick.

The creaking steel door lifted his head as the correction officer stood there with Kevin Cook, all decked out in an orange jumpsuit accessorized with chrome leggings and bracelets. He was one angry man.

"Really, Officer. Do we need that?" Jerry asked pointing to the shackles. "He's not going anywhere."

The CO shrugged his shoulders and removed the bindings from his inmate. "There you go. Good luck." Kevin's color shed one layer of anger.

Kevin Cook sat down across from Jerry. The desk was so small they were face to face. "I guess you're my lawyer," Kevin said. "Fancy briefcase."

"You guessed right," Jerry said reaching out and shaking his new client's hand.

"I didn't do nothin," Kevin blurted out. "It's a frame. A hoax. I have a witness."

"I'm sure it is, Mr. Cook." *Except that witness is about to throw you under the bus.* "That's what you have me for."

"What about bail?"

"That's a good news–bad news thing. They have set bail. But it's a hundred thousand dollars."

"What?" he screamed. "Where's the good news in that? Who has that kind of money?"

"I know," said Jerry in a calm voice. "Not many. Do you have friends or family that can help?"

Kevin's color went up two shades of anger. "No," he mumbled.

"Sorry. It is what it is."

"You can't do any better than that?"

"It's a whole lot less than what the prosecutor asked for, Kevin. Yes, it's the best we can do. I know how you feel . . ."

"How could you know how I feel? Yer not wear'n this Halloween costume look'n like the Great Pumpkin."

"I know. Settle down. That's the last of your worries. We have important things to talk about." He paused until Kevin seemed to come to grips with his situation.

"OK," he said. "Go ahead. Wudda we have?"

"Well, of course you have the previous charges of assaulting a police officer, Battery of a Minor, a small narcotics charge and a new one, Aggravated Battery of a Minor."

Kevin scoffed. "What's that one?"

"Apparently, the night your wife left, Carl Cook was left half beaten to death and claims you did it."

"He's a liar," scoffed Kevin.

"Whatever. As serious as those are, they aren't our highest priority. They can be plead out. This last one is our priority. There are only three options in the State of Maine—murder, felony murder, and manslaughter. They have charged you with murder."

Kevin smirked. "You're not going to ask me if I done it?"

"You just said you didn't. I have no reason to believe otherwise. But whether you say you did or you say you didn't, that doesn't change the defense. The only thing the jury is going to care about is the evidence. And they have a lot of circumstantial evidence. Abuse . . ."

"I didn't abuse nobody," he interrupted. "That bastard kid just done that to get back at me."

"Get back at you for what?" asked Jerry.

"To get my house. Get my money. He's just carrying a grudge because I taught him to be tough."

"Well, what about all these medical reports for both him and your wife?"

"I can't help it if they's all clumsy."

"Well, these types of injuries might take more of an explanation than that," said Jerry. He had heard all this stuff before. "Let' just go over your story of the night she left."

"Simple. It's the same thing I told that detective. Sure, we had a little scuffle. She didn't tell me she was going to leave. She was going to sneak out of the house. I caught her. Shouldn't be any surprise I was angry."

"How angry?"

"Not angry enough to do what they said I done," he replied. "The boy called the police. They was no need for that. You'll get the same story from Charley. I let her go after I calmed down."

"Tell me about your relationship with Charley."

"We've known each other since we was kids. On the baseball team together. We were state champs," he said flashing a little glow that didn't flicker very long.

"So, you are buddies?"

"I guess you could say that."

"Well, that doesn't help as far as his testimony goes. The jury will scrutinize what he says. Was Susan planning on taking Carl with her?"

"I don't know. She didn't."

"Why? Weren't they close?"

"I don't know. She didn't birth him. She dopted him. And she never told'm. Maybe she wer'nt as close as she pretended."

"That's interesting," said Jerry rubbing his chin. "That's not in the file."

"Check it out. He wasn't no more her blood than mine. Goes to show you what liars they all is."

"I will. That helps. Let's talk about the bat. The prosecution believes there was a bat that you used to kill her and now it's missing. Where is it?"

"I don't know. I told them it got stole. Maybe the kid. I didn't give him no money. He had to make do on his own. Maybe he decided it was quick cash."

"It sure would help our case if we could find that and dispel the myth. But if it's gone, it's gone. Let's go over the timeline. What time did Officer Wickes show up at the house?"

"I dunno. After ten. I was too upset to be looking at any old clock."

"Maybe you remember some things after you calmed down. What time did the officer leave?"

"I guess round eleven."

"And what time did Susan leave?"

Kevin hesitated. "I'm not sure."

"Before or after Officer Wickes left?" More hesitation. "It's an important detail, Kevin. You know that Wickes is going to say he didn't see her leave and that it was after he was gone."

"After," grunted Kevin.

Under the bus, buddy, thought the counsel, *under the bus*. "OK. What else do you have that will help our case?"

"I told ya the truth, all of it. That's all I can do," he replied.

"OK," Jerry said, "let me ask you this. The odds are not exactly in our favor. Particularly when we have Carl Cook's testimony that will refute yours and Officer Wickes's. And Officer Wickes says he wasn't around when she left. That leaves you on the hook by yourself. If it were possible for the prosecution to lower the charge to manslaughter, is that something to which you would consider pleading guilty?"

"I told ya, I didn't do it," he snapped.

Pride goes before destruction. Happens all the time, thought the defender as he reassured his client, "I have to ask. OK, then. We're going all the way."

He shook his hand and beckoned for the correction officer. "We'll be talking."

§§§

Two angry men. The second one was Officer Wickes busted down to desk duty until the trial was over. The station was giving him an old fashioned Amish shunning as if they had all suddenly gotten religion. It was clear that if Kevin Cook was found guilty, Charley Wickes would be the next to fall. Chief Sullivan was already planning an expedited retirement without any fanfare.

Jerry Moss waited in the interview room for Charley. They all looked the same. Cube shaped. Depressing colors. Dim lighting. Cheap table. Metal chairs. The eerie mirror always gave him the creeps.

Charley opened the door to see the young lawyer sitting there in his suit and shiny briefcase. He wasn't impressed.

"Officer," said Jerry reaching out his hand, "nice to meet you."

Charley grunted and sat down. "Let's get this over with," he said leaning the chair back on two legs.

"No problem. We just need to go over your testimony. I have the transcripts from your original interview with Detective Small."

Charley rolled his eyes. "Well, don't put too much credence in what he says. He ain't to be trusted, believe me. You know why he left Boston?" he asked teeing it up quickly. "They threw him out. Evidence tampering. Check it out."

I did. Squeaky clean. "I'll do that. Nevertheless, we still have to answer to what you said on tape. That can't be redacted. So, let's start with the 9–1–1 call. How was it you were the one dispatched and not someone else?"

"What's that got to do with it?" he asked bringing the chair down on all fours.

"We have to anticipate questions the prosecution will ask. The fact that you two have a history together will make them want to suggest a conspiracy. You took the call so you could cover for your buddy."

Charley's face was turning darker by the second. "I was the one on duty that night. That simple."

"Weren't there a couple other deputies patrolling on that shift?" he asked.

"Maybe, but I was obviously the closest one to the incident being called in."

First lie, thought the lawyer as he continued his questioning. "OK. You know they will check the logs on everyone else out there that night. So you arrived sometime after ten o'clock. Walk me through the rest of the timeline."

"Sure. One more time. I arrived. It was a simple domestic dispute. I calmed both of them down as I was trained. I left."

"Alright. The prosecution will drill into that a lot deeper, so let's go over some details. Was Susan Cook injured at all when you arrived?"

"No. They had been shoving each other. I think she was on the floor but no injuries."

Think she was on the floor. "Did he have a bat in his hands?"

"No."

"Now you know that will be refuted by the prosecution's witness."

"The kid's a liar."

"Well, we'll certainly question him and, if so, it will come out. Where was Susan Cook when you left?"

"She was in the bathroom getting herself fixed up to leave."

"So, she was roughed up a bit?"

"Uh . . . no. I think she was trying to regain her composure."

"And what time did you leave?"

"What my log says. Around eleven o'clock."

"That's about an hour. The prosecution will wonder what took an hour given the short version of events you just gave me."

"I can't help that. It took a while to get them talking. To find out what the issue was. She wanted to leave. He didn't want her to. He had to reconcile the fact that he couldn't stop her."

"That's a good answer. But we still have to address this version of events with what you have on tape with Detective Small. You said in that interrogation that you saw Susan Cook drive away. Now you are saying she was still in the house when you left."

"It was a long time ago. That so-called detective was firing questions so fast just to get me off track. After I had time to think about the details, I remembered that she hadn't left that fast."

"You know that puts your buddy hanging out there by himself." *Called throwing your buddy under the bus.*

"I can't testify to something I didn't see. He'll have to deal with it."

"OK. It is what it is. Carl Cook. He was severely injured that night, whether or not you know how it occurred. What do you know about that?"

"Nothing. He wasn't there when I arrived or when I left."

"And Kevin said nothing about Carl? He was, after all, the one who called the disturbance in."

"Just that he got scared and ran and fell out the back door."

"But no one thought to go look for him?"

"Guess not. He wasn't part of my investigation."

"I see. One last thing," said Jerry. "The bat. The prosecution wants that badly. Do you have any idea where it is right now?"

Charley started fidgeting with his fingers. "No idea. He says it was stolen."

"Alright," finished the lawyer standing up and shaking his hand. "We'll go over the testimony one more time before the trial." *Which hopefully there won't be. We're toast.*

XXV

PERRY RICHARDSON drummed his fingers on the desk as Robin Peters sat across from him with her hands folded.

"Sir, you're call just came through."

"Thanks, Donna. I'll take it now," he replied. The phone buzzed. "This is Perry."

"Hi, Perry. This is Liz. How are you doing?"

"We're doing well. Hope you are too. I have Robin here also."

"Hi, Robin. Yes, I'm doing great."

"Hi, Liz."

"Well like I said in the email, I have some exciting news so I'll get right to it. It's a good news–bad news thing. Good news first. I found out where Susan moved. She remarried to a man named Kevin Cook. Her son's name is Carl Cook and he lives in Woodspring, Maine."

"That's wonderful," said Perry. "Wait . . . Woodspring? That's where David lives!"

"I know. I saw him there and talked to him. He had no idea that Carl was Deborah's son until just recently."

"How did you find them? How did you see David in Woodspring? How is it he just found out?"

Liz was silent for a second. Perry could immediately sense the impending somber tenor. "Well, that's the bad news part. I found her in the obituaries."

"The obituaries?"

Perry and Robin looked like they didn't know what end to pick up first.

"Yes," she said. "She was murdered. About a year ago. They just arrested her husband for the crime." She then went through all the details she knew.

"So, where is Carl?" asked Perry. "Where is he living? Who is taking care of him?"

"Well, he's living by himself."

"What? You have to be kidding!"

"It's not as bad as it seems. This was apparently his choice and since he met the requirements, they had no reason to stop him. But please don't be too worried. He has a lot of support. David is keeping a close eye on him, but also the detective that is investigating the case has taken an unusually keen interest in him. Between the two of them, I think he is OK."

"Maybe so, but it doesn't make me very comfortable."

"Well, I gave your contact information to Detective Luke Small. He is going to call you this afternoon to discuss Carl. And he is also working a warrant with Les Enfants to find the girl. We certainly don't need one anymore for Carl."

"I was wondering who else was searching. Nate Bourassa, and by the way, you were right. He is so nice to work with. Anyway, he said there were actually two other inquiries looking for Carl. This detective is one, but I don't know who the third party would be."

"So how is that going?" asked Liz.

"We served the warrant. That was no problem. We got the documents. Of course we knew about Susan. We just didn't know where she was and what her name had changed to. But we do have a problem on locating the parents of the girl. They had their names redacted. That's not unusual if they don't want the birth parents showing up. There are ways around it, but it takes time."

"Oh, I wish I could help you."

"Well, Mr. Bourassa wouldn't tell me who the third party was, but he said a meeting might be arranged in Bangor that would answer everyone's questions. He's going to call me back."

"That sounds encouraging. I guess I can't do anymore, but I do hope you will let me know how it all works out."

"I will, Liz. I can't thank you enough. And I'm going to give David a call."

"I'm sure he's expecting it. Don't forget. Detective Small will be calling you. He is really a great person and I'm sure will give you the confidence that Carl is in good hands."

"I hope so. Thanks again."

§§§

Luke Small sat with his chin resting on one hand like The Thinker only he wasn't thinking. He had rolled this around so much in his mind it was as tasteless as gum that had been chewed too long. Eva sat across from him at a loss how to help.

"Should I say anything?" he asked one more time.

"I don't know. The odds of this happening are astronomical."

"Maybe. But we've all seen these true life stories of long lost relatives finding each other in odd places at the same time. Remember that story of two sisters that were adopted across the country from each other and ended up working at the same hospital in Florida? Mr. Bourassa was as helpful as he could be but there is nothing he can do about the adoption papers. The adoptive and birth parents of the girl were redacted. I pulled Kathy's adoption papers out of the safe. Guess what?"

"Redacted?"

"Yes. Same adoption agency. Essentially the same birthday, just a few minutes after midnight. Obviously we didn't redact our names, but the birth parent's names were redacted. It's possible the parents are the same for Kathy and Carl. The only reason we used Les Enfants is that is where Kristy was from. That's where we met. It's nerve racking."

"I understand. But still. Won't you know for sure soon?"

"I hope so. Sarah is calling every day. I just can't see her hurt. She was all I had when Kristy died. We have been through it together." He looked into Eva's eyes and smiled. "And now I have you, too."

That remark was immediately met with a look that melted him to the core. Luke wanted to get down on one knee right then and there. But that wasn't the plan. Christmas. Kathy had it all scripted. To be spontaneous, of course.

"I know it's making you crazy. But you said this Nathan Bourassa was slipping hints to you that there was a resolution."

"Yes, he did. And when I talked to Perry Richardson, he said the same thing. Mr. Bourassa wouldn't come right out and say it, but I got a strong feeling that this third party is interested in Carl's adoption. That could be Mr. Castello, Carl's birth father, but that's unlikely after all this time. Or it could be the girl's adoptive parents who want to know more about her twin brother. That would be the best case. And if it is the adoptive parents, why, after all these years, would they suddenly be interested in finding her twin brother."

"See. You're the detective. I agree. It makes sense. I think you are worrying for nothing. How could they keep the adoptive parents name secret if you and Kristy were the adoptive parents?"

"You wouldn't believe all the things out there I've seen that don't make sense. That's what gives detectives job security, sorting it all out."

"I know you'll get all the answers."

"I don't doubt that. It's just the timing. Mr. Bourassa said it would be best if all the parties could meet at his office in Bangor. He suggested strongly that if we set up the meeting, this mystery party might be there. You're right. It would have to be the girl's parents. Who else would it be? Thanks for making me feel better." But he didn't.

"How soon will this meeting take place?"

"Getting Perry and whoever the other party together will probably take a week. I'm ready to drive up there at a moment's notice. I just don't know if I can wait. Perry is setting it up."

There was a knock on the door. Luke looked up to see Sarah with yet another file.

"Come in, Sarah," he said.

"Hi, Eva," she said with a wink.

"Hi, Sarah. How are you?"

"Doing better," she said as she placed the file squarely in front of the detective and stood there waiting with her arms crossed and a little smirk.

Luke looked up at her. "This is it?"

She nodded.

Luke slowly opened the file and carefully studied the results. His eyes opened wide as two full moons as the first smile in days spread across his face.

"Thanks, Sarah. I can breathe again."

"You're welcome."

"See," said Eva.

XXVI

IT WAS six o'clock. The sun had clocked out two hours ago. David and Mary started their drive to Woodspring High school. The play started at seven o'clock. She wanted to get a seat down front. They might as well have been riding in separate vehicles.

"I guess the good news is it won't be long before the days start getting longer," said David to break the silence. "Before you know it, we won't be able to see all these stars until five, and then six.

"Tell me again what he said," asked Mary as if not hearing him.

"He was very gracious. He said he would give it some thought. The boy has a mind of his own. That I can tell you."

"Like someone I know. But he can't live out in the woods like a hermit by himself. He still has two and half years of high school. He needs someone to guide him, help him. A mother."

"He's going to need time to process all the drama in his life. I think we do too. He doesn't really know us and it's not like he's used to anyone reaching out to him."

"Well, you already reached out to him, to help him in his studies."

"I'm glad I did. That will help him warm up. That doesn't undo all the time he was marginalized. It takes time to build trust. We have to be patient. I think I know him. He'll come around."

"But Christmas is coming up in a week. He needs a family to be with."

"Why are you so obsessed with the boy?" asked David looking over at his wife's dejected face.

"I don't know," she replied. "There's just something about him. He's a wonderful boy."

"I think he is too," he said. "I can see the longing in your eyes. Is it because you see him as the son we never had? That's my fault, not wanting to adopt. . ."

"It's not your fault, David. You carry too much weight on your shoulders and you keep piling it on. Like your sister's death. Maybe you were having an argument when she had her accident, but that has nothing to do with someone running a red light. It couldn't be helped. I could have made more of an issue about adopting. I'm as much responsible as you. I don't know why I didn't. Maybe I was scared too. But this boy is different. Maybe I do see him as the son we didn't have. Even if it's only for a couple years. And what a wonderful mentor you would be."

David drove on quietly. The high school lights came into view. He pulled into the faculty parking lot to his regular space and put it in park. He kept the car running as he stared out at the stars."

"Aren't we going in?" she asked.

"Oh . . . yes, of course. There are a couple things I need to share with you first."

"What?"

"I've been doing some investigating of my own. You're right. I take on weights that only I can take credit for. Do you remember all that home nurse care and all that equipment we had before your operation?"

"Yes."

"We never got a bill. Did you ever wonder why?"

"No. Only that you were concerned about it."

"Our insurance didn't cover any of it. I called again to find out if we were going to get a bill. There won't be. It was all paid in full. Deborah . . . she paid every penny out of her own pocket." David fumbled for the words.

"Oh, honey," she said stroking his arm.

"I know. That argument I had with her . . . the last words spoken. Calling her selfish and greedy. I was so wrong. She was so much more than I knew in my ignorance. Even if I can't forgive myself, she would have."

"Oh, I know. I know Deborah. She would and she did."

"Well, there is a lot more to the story than that."

"What could that be? That was a lot."

"I thought it a little strange this attraction you had for Carl. It seemed like there had to be more to it. I called Dr. Maxey to see if I could find out who the heart donor was. He directed me to the appropriate people. It was not kept a secret."

Mary's eyes opened wide and instantaneously glassed over. "You're kidding?"

"No. Perry directed Deborah's heart to go specifically to you."

They just stared into each other's eyes, tears now trickling.

"Her life for mine," Mary said under her breath.

David nodded and then bowed his head. They held hands for a few minutes in silent prayer.

"Ready?" he asked.

"Ready."

§§§

"What does break a leg even mean?" asked Carl.

"An idiom for good luck?" suggested Kathy.

"Wishing someone harm is a good luck? Thespian minds must be warped."

They chuckled quietly. The night before the two week Christmas break, the auditorium was filling up.

What have I gotten myself into? thought Carl standing behind the curtain and feeling suddenly ridiculous in full makeup and costume. He was always comfortable in the shadows. The bright lights were something new. *Writers don't have to subject themselves to public humiliation. They can at least use a pen name.*

Kathy rubbed his back. "Just opening night jitters," she said.

"And closing night ones too, thankfully," he replied.

"They say a bad dress rehearsal means a good opening night," Kathy laughed. "We should have a pretty good night."

"That's for sure. It was pretty bad. Somehow, that doesn't give me much confidence."

He could see David and Mary sitting in the front row directly in the center. Luke and Eva were a few rows back. It looked like a capacity crowd. *All the more to make a fool of myself.*

Ready or not, the show must go on. Mrs. Slip kept a tight schedule and at seven o'clock, not a minute less and not a minute more, she stepped out in front of the curtain to introduce her personally abridged version of Julius Caesar.

And hence, without further ado, the curtain went up. Flavius stood on stage with the first line, "Hence! home, you idle creatures get you home . . ."

Carl waited for Scene Two. The slow but unceasing time was not his friend. Finally the curtain went up and there was no more hiding of Carl's debut.

"Calpurnia!" he called.

The simple line at least allowed him to clear his throat and cool his nervousness. As the scene went on, he could see Mary staring at him. It was the same endearing way as at the wake. She was so close, it felt like she was part of the play. His mind swerved to his conversation with David earlier in the day. Suddenly he heard someone behind the curtain handing him a line. He looked out over the waiting crowd.

Pay attention, idiot! "Forget not, in your speed, Antonius, . . ." *Hurry up and kill me Brutus.* "To touch Calpurnia; for our elders say, the barren, touched in this holy chase, shake off their sterile curse."

Carl had looked forward to Act III which would put him out of his misery, but now he had mixed feelings. *Maybe this isn't so bad. Kind of fun.*

But he had to die and Andy had to do it. "Et tu, Brute! Then fall, Caesar." And Carl fell to the floor.

Andy had gotten over his fear of killing Carl and Caesar was no more. Carl enjoyed the rest of the show from behind the set as he watched his friend steal the show.

The cast showed nothing but Cheshire Cat teeth as the curtain rose to a standing ovation. Flowers flowed to giddy performers. Eva handed Kathy and Carl a dozen roses each. Andy drew the greatest applause. He deserved it.

They scrubbed the bulk of the makeup off their faces to get as quickly as possible to their favorite pizza place. Andy was already there gushing in his newfound fame. Two junior high girls came over and asked him for his autograph. He obliged with glee.

"Your pizza is getting cold, Andy. With many more plays like this", said Carl, "you'll be down to skin and bones."

"And what about the Tin Man, here?" laughed Andy. "Looks like Caesar rusted up for a moment. He was easy to kill."

Carl blushed.

"And that look on your face," said Kathy. "Where in the world did you go?"

"I'll tell you later," he replied taking a big bite of pizza.

Mouths full of pizza didn't stop anyone from interjecting their version of events at any crack in the conversation. Carl wondered if he should practice the Heimlich Maneuver in case they started choking while they were talking.

After that last basketball game, Bobby Martin and Judy Wickes weren't feeling quite as jubilant. They sat in a corner away from the festivities firing off sullen looks as if anyone cared. No one did.

All good things come to an end, they say. This night was subject to the same laws. No school for two weeks didn't mean they could stay out all night. Carl drove Kathy home. It was close to midnight. The lights were on. He walked her to the door.

"That was so much fun, wasn't it?" she asked.

He just looked at her. "You're so much fun," he said. He leaned over and kissed her. She let it linger this time.

"Good night," he said. "What time did your father want to come over and cut down that Christmas tree?"

"He'll want it to warm up some. Probably around noon."

"I'll have lunch ready, then," he said.

"That should be interesting."

He just smiled.

The drive home seemed lonelier this time. The pines swayed in the breeze casting eerie shadows in the moonlight like tall thin unwelcoming hosts. His mind couldn't contain one more thought. There was the frivolity of his new friends. There was Kathy, and now David McKinley wanted him to come live with him. *Does he really want me?* he wondered. *Or does he just feel sorry for the pitiful orphan? Or is it the new nephew connection? Guilt? Duty? His wife looks sincere although she hasn't said so much as a word. There's an odd familiarity to her face. Luke has offered also. That would be awkward with Kathy.* He started up his gravel driveway. The old house had one stark yellow bulb glowing on the front porch. Nothing about it said home.

They're right. I can't stay out here forever. He parked his SUV, turned the key in the front door and turned up the furnace. He sat down in the living room. Everything about the place was cold, almost foreboding. *No. I have to go.*

Carl got ready for bed. It was all rote. He couldn't remember if he brushed his teeth, but the toothbrush lay wet in the holder. He lay down hoping to come down from the evening's high, but it had a long way to drop. His mind rambled for an hour until nothing was making sense. When it finally wore itself out, sweet sleep started to cuddle him. So did something else.

His eyes snapped open as his nostrils choked for air. Smoke! The room was filled with heavy smoke. He ripped the covers off and got low to the floor. He crawled on all fours to the hallway. The entire downstairs was in flames. There was no exit. The smoke got thicker. It was hard to breath. He coughed with each breath. He crawled back to his room. He could feel the heat enveloping the old house. The window wouldn't open. He stood up and threw a lamp stand through the glass. He could feel the back draft as flames exploded behind him.

He stuck his head out the window, finally gasping some air. The whole house was in flames. All the way around each side. He took a sheet to clear away the broken glass. He didn't have time to make a rope out of sheets. It was jump or die. It was a convincing argument.

He hit the ground and rolled away from the house. The pain seared his leg as he crawled away. He could see a shadow lit up by the flames just behind the tree line. Carl stared at the figure. It seemed uncertain whether to come toward Carl or run. It ran.

XXVII

THE COOK house lit up the night sky like a Roman Candle. It was Jumbo Keme who saw the light from his cabin and called it in. That one hundred year old tinder box burned to the ground so fast that all the Fire Department had when they arrived was a pile of ashes. But the last ashes did not go cold until two days later. That's how long it took three cords of unused, well-seasoned wood residing in the basement to finally burn out.

It was Jumbo for the second time who came to save his childhood friend. Not waiting for the paramedics, he took him to the hospital. They set the compound fracture on his left leg and treated him for minor burns and smoke inhalation. Luke sped from the hospital back to the scene. He was in good hands.

Whoever the arsonist was, they bungled the attempt to hide their tracks. Most of the gas cans were burned in the fire, but a couple lay on the ground as if they ran out of time to destroy all the evidence. According to the Fire Chief, the arsonist must have had access to the inside of the house. The flames started both inside and out clearly to make short work of the fire and block anyone from escaping. The question was who.

Charley Wickes was playing poker late into the night with what friends he had left. Kevin Cook had the perfect alibi. Detective Luke Small walked around the grounds looking for clues.

"What kind of a track is that?" he asked Chris Blaise.

Chris got down on a knee and examined it. "I don't know. I wouldn't call it a store bought boot."

"It goes off into the woods, but disappears. Who do we have that's a tracker?"

"Charley Wickes," Chris said.

"Yeah . . . that probably won't work. Let's get these gas cans to the lab. See if there are any prints or anyway to track who bought them. They look new."

"Yes, sir," said Chris.

Luke walked around the property in circles. There had to be more clues. There always were. Concentration was difficult. His mind kept gravitating to Carl. *I said I would take care of him.*

He would be safe. I let him down. This was about worst case. How did this happen? No wonder he doesn't trust us. He has made such progress, and now this. Who was patrolling last night? Where were they when this happened? There should have only been an hour to pull this off before they rolled by again. Who would know the schedule? The detective thumped himself in the head. Wickes.

The detective walked back over to the tracks he had found heading for the tree line. Officer Blaise was pouring a plaster cast of the depression. *Who else can we get? Someone who might recognize a boot print like this. A hunter, trapper, fisherman maybe. Someone who knows the woods,* thought the detective. *Unlike us city folk.* Suddenly it dawned on him. *There have to be plenty of woodsmen around here, and I know at least one.*

"Chris. Take over. I'll be right back," he said as he jumped in his cruiser and spun gravel down the road.

Luke pulled up in the driveway and knocked on the door.

"Detective. What can I do for you?" asked Principal Nick Thompson.

"Mr. Thompson, you promised to show me the way of the woods once. Do you remember?"

"I do," he said.

The detective just stood there staring, waiting as if it was understood.

"Now? Seriously? Before breakfast?"

"How would you like to do a good thing?"

"Of course."

"Then now would be a good time. Care to go for a ride?"

"Sure. Can you tell me where you want to go?"

"The Cook house went up in flames last night."

"Oh, I'm sorry to hear that. Did anyone get hurt?"

"Some injuries, but the good news is Carl escaped with his life. It was arson. We found some odd tracks disappearing into the brush. I was looking for somebody that might be able to identify what they were and even track them. I sure don't."

"Give me a second. Come on in. I think I can help you. Carrie, please get the detective a cup of coffee while I get my stuff."

Carrie brought a black cup of coffee. "You guys work pretty early for a Saturday morning."

"Thanks, ma'am. Crime knows no time."

Luke took one sip when Nick Thompson was back in full gear and boots. "Let's go."

He's no nonsense, that's for sure, thought Luke. *Me neither.* He hit the road with lights flashing, siren blaring, and speed limits removed until he came to a skidding halt in Carl's driveway.

"That was a trip," smiled the principal getting out of the car. "That got the blood flowing." He looked at the smoking remains. "Wow . . . that must have gone up like a match book."

"It was ripe, for sure," said Luke marching toward the start of the footprints.

Nick Thompson followed Luke to the tree line. Luke pointed out his evidence.

"These are homemade moccasins," said Nick, "either deer hide or moose hide. There are a few Indians around that still make them and even fewer mountain men."

"Mountain men?"

"Yeah. There are still some around. They're hermits, trappers. Whatever you want to call them. They live off the land, off the grid for sure. Let's go," said Nick as he pulled out a machete.

I am beginning to like this guy after all, thought Luke. He stayed right behind Nick as he pointed out things he never would have seen, mostly broken branches and disturbed leaves. Nick would pick a footprint occasionally. They chopped their way for a while like jungle explorers until they came out on a path. Nick stopped for a second to catch his breath and wipe his brow.

"Got to get some of this weight off," he said. "These are deer trails. They network all through these woods. We won't need this anymore," he said to Luke as he sheathed his machete and wiped his brow.

Luke looked down at his muddy scratched up shoes. "Good," he said.

"See the tracks?" asked Nick. "They'll be easy to follow now."

Luke followed closely behind Nick as he navigated the woods as if the trail were marked. After about an hour, Nick said, "I know where this is going."

"You do? Where?"

"There aren't that many that know the woods this well. Actually, there's only one in this area. Arnold MacDonald. They call him Mack. He lives out here by himself. The only money he makes is off poaching. Or other activities."

"What other activities?"

"Nothing legal from what I hear. But they're only rumors."

They continued on for another half mile to a small clearing in the woods. The trail ended at a tiny shack of a cabin expelling a plume of white smoke. Someone was in there.

"This is where we have to be careful," said Nick lowering his voice and ducking down. "This guy is dangerous. If I were you, I wouldn't consider knocking on that door without backup. And don't let him see us. He would have no problem picking us off."

"What's with that little dozer parked by the cabin?"

"I don't know. He doesn't do any work for these loggers."

"Looks like he's moved a lot of dirt around," Luke said. "Can't be doing that for the fun of it."

"Good point," said Nick. "I'd be scared to see what's in those mounds."

"OK, we need to back track," said Luke proud that he might have said something woodsman like. "We can come back. Are there any roads to this place or are they just trails?"

"There are plenty of logging roads. I can get us back."

"Good. Thanks, Nick. I don't know if you realize what you've just done for us."

Nicks face gleamed with redemption.

"Also, hate to act like a city boy, but do we have to go back the way we came?"

Nick laughed quietly. "No, there is an easier way."

§§§

Ben Keme decided to stay home this weekend after getting a call from Jumbo. The smell of burning sausage returned his attention to the stove. He quickly turned them over in hopes of saving some of it. Carl was stretched out on the sofa with his cast resting on the floor. Jumbo was retrieving some eggs from the refrigerator.

"Tell me again, Carl," said Ben, "what happened. Why did you have to jump?"

"The fire was everywhere," said Carl. "It happened so fast. There was no way out."

"How long were you asleep?"

"I wasn't really. Just starting to doze off. I think that's how I made it out at all."

"Did you smell gas or anything?"

"Now that you mention it, I did just before I started to doze."

"But you didn't hear anything?"

"No. Nothing."

"And you say you saw someone in the woods watching?"

"Yes. I'm sure of it. He hesitated. I didn't know if he was coming to save me or finish me off. Then he turned and disappeared."

"Finish you off," said Jumbo with no uncertainty.

"Anything about him you can remember? What he was wearing?" asked Ben.

"It was just a shadow. It did look like he had one of those overcoats with the fringe hanging down like Buffalo Bill."

"Hmmm . . . interesting," said Ben.

"Do you know who it was?" asked Jumbo.

"I have an idea," replied Ben. It wasn't Wickes. I know where his card game was. He's been doing a lot of mouthing lately, usually when he gets drunk. Which they say he's been doing more often."

They all seemed to be in an analytical state as Ben cracked the eggs into the sausage grease. It spit and crackled into that famous aroma distracting them for a short while. Carl clumsily used his crutches to get to the kitchen table. Jumbo popped open a beer. Ben gave him a look.

"Hey, it's Saturday," said Jumbo.

"Maybe so, brother. But it might be time to put on the war paint and be sober."

Jumbo looked over at his brother as if receiving a secret code.

"Gotcha," Jumbo said replacing the beer with a glass of milk.

"War paint?" asked Carl. "I guess it is war."

"Make no mistake about it, Carl. I've been there and I know what it looks like. There is no doubt someone wants you dead. It's obvious who is behind it. Eat up. We need to prepare."

Carl wolfed down his food. "Prepare for what?"

"You'll see," replied Ben.

They finished in silence and let the dishes set. Ben nodded at Jumbo. Ben walked over to the wall and removed his shotgun as Jumbo walked into the bedroom. Carl's head whirled. *What's this all about?*

Jumbo came back with a black garbage bag that held some thin object. The throat of the bag had been sealed with duct tape.

Ben cleared the table and put some plastic over it. "Show him," he said.

Jumbo peeled the duct tape off the opening. Then he put some gloves on. With two fingers he pulled it out and laid it on the table.

Carl's eyes opened wide enough for them to fall out. "Wha . . . what?" Then they rolled back in his head as they played a flashback.

There in front of him was a bat with Ted Williams' signature almost completely illegible for all the splattered blood.

"Where did you get this?" asked Carl.

Ben's head wheeled around as he heard a car come up to the house. He grabbed the shotgun and peered out the window trying not to be seen.

"Hold off on the story," Ben said. "Let's tell it one time." He set the shotgun in the corner.

Ben opened the door before there was a knock. "Come on in, Detective. I'm Ben. I don't think we've met."

Luke shook his hand. "Nice to meet you, Ben. Carl's said good things about you. Hi, Jumbo." Then he saw Carl sitting at the table with the bat and he froze in his tracks. "Carl . . ."

"Carl has only known about this for two minutes. He didn't know we had it. Jumbo was just getting ready to explain. Please sit."

Luke put his hands on Carl's shoulders. "How are you doing, Carl?"

"I'm OK, considering," he replied.

Luke sat down. "I'm all ears."

Jumbo looked over at Carl. "That night you crawled over here half dead. I took you to the hospital. Then I hiked over to your house."

"Why?" asked Carl.

Jumbo just looked at him. "I was going to finish it," he said looking sideways at the detective.

"Finish it? What does that mean?"

"What's the word? Naive? That's what I love about you, Carl. I mean end it."

"Don't worry, Jumbo," said Luke. "Nobody is taking a confession. You didn't do it. Let's just stay with what actually happened."

"Thank you, sir. When I got there, it was about three in the morning, there was a lot of activity going on in the house. You could smell bleach clear out where I was hiding."

"Who was there?" asked Luke.

"Charley Wickes and Kevin. Then a third person came out of the woods. He talked to them a while and then got in Carl's mother's car and drove it off."

"Just came out of the woods?" asked Luke.

"We can give you an idea of who that was," said Ben. "He may have made another visit last night."

"Anyway," continued Jumbo, "he drove off in the car and then Charley came out and drove off in his cruiser. I waited for about an hour and then snuck in the house. Kevin was drunk on the floor with the bat lying beside him. I was getting ready to . . ."

"You don't have to go there," said Luke, "just tell me what you did, not what you *thought* you wanted to do."

"Right. OK, so I decided to take the bat."

"Why?" asked Luke. "Why not call the . . . forget it."

"Insurance," said Ben.

"But why didn't you try to get it to some other authorities. You don't think Chief Sullivan . . ."

"Sorry, Detective. Not to offend you, but we are surrounded by pale faces," said Ben. "Redskins, as they call us when they're nice, don't just walk into a police station and expect to be listened to."

"I understand. I am assuming you are now ready to enter this into my custody?"

"Yes, sir." said Ben.

"If this provides the information I think it does, it will be over, Carl," said Luke.

Luke could see some of the tension flow out of Carl as he leaned back in his chair. But there was still a ways to go.

"You said you thought you might have an idea who the third person was? I think I do too."

"Mack," said Ben.

"We're pretty sure he was the arsonist. We're picking him up as we speak."

"That's good," said Ben. "Finally."

"Carl, I was hoping you would come back with me. I can see you have some friends here that can't be replaced. I'll understand whatever your decision is. Also, David McKinley called me when he heard about the fire. He and his wife are very upset and concerned. He said he talked to you yesterday about living with them?"

Carl looked over at Jumbo. "Go," said Jumbo. "You won't be safe here until they're all locked up."

"OK," he said using a crutch to climb up. He gave Jumbo and Ben a hug. "Real friends. The real deal. But I'm not leaving without one of those burned sausages." He stuffed one in his mouth.

"It's all good, Kemosabi," said Jumbo laughing.

Carl laughed too. It hurt. Luke put his coat around Carl's shoulders and helped him to the cruiser. He put the crutches in the back seat.

"Where to?" he asked.

"Uncle David," he said.

"Maybe someone you want to see first?"

Carl smiled. "Yes. Maybe we could stop somewhere and buy a shirt? Jumbo's pants are perfect for this cast, but the rest, not so much."

"You bet."

XXVIII

IT IS said that the day a child is born, a mother is also born. If that is true, then it is equally true that when a child dies, so also does the mother. Nancy Campbell, then, was at death's door as she held the hand of her daughter. The devil has many names. They often have a Latin etymology like Acute Lymphoblastic Leukemia but, like their namesake, they have one thing in common—consuming just one is never enough. They want to consume everyone in close proximity.

"Don't look so sad," said Zoey.

"My beautiful girl," she said rubbing her bald head.

"Sure, Mom. Are you going to give me that bald is beautiful line again?"

"It's true," she replied kissing her on the head. "If anyone could make all us women want to shave their heads, it would be you."

Zoey tried to laugh but it came out a cough.

"You just rest," said her mother. She looked up at the doctor beckoning an answer with her eyes.

"Good news. The fever is coming down," Dr. David said as he scribbled one more entry in her chart. "We need to keep an eye on her until it subsides completely. Her immune system is getting weaker."

"Tell me again why that bone marrow didn't transplant work?" she asked. "I thought it was so promising."

"I thought so also, Nancy. There just never are any guarantees, no good answer. It worked well for quite a while. That's the good news. It buys us time. If there is a brother out there, we have a fifty percent chance of getting a positive match."

"Wouldn't the chances be higher with a twin?"

"No. Sorry. If they were identical twins, yes. But not fraternal. The possibility of a match is the same as any other sibling."

"What about her biological father?"

"Certainly worth pursuing but the odds are unlikely since the mother was such a good match."

"Thank you, Doctor," she said retaking her seat by her daughter.

"I'll be back later this afternoon to check on her," he said and walked out.

"Just think, Mom," said Zoey, "I might get to meet my real brother, twin brother no less. How exciting is that?"

Nancy just smiled. *What a bright star she is. Always giving us hope when it should be us lifting her up*, she thought. *We can't let this light go out.*

But it was more of a shooting star.

"What's the matter, sweetie?"

"Deborah. I was just thinking of her. It brought back my sad feeling. Wasn't she something?"

"She was, dear, she was." *She really was. Not at all what I expected. Gracious. Loving. Giving. I feared her interfering in our lives for no reason. If anything, she enhanced them.*

"It was such a short time to know her. I'll never be able to talk to her again. I just miss her."

"I know, honey," she said holding her hand. "It makes me sad too."

"When is Daddy going to call?"

"Soon . . . soon. Mr. Bourassa was very optimistic about the meeting. He couldn't believe that so many inquiries came all at once searching for you and your brother. Just when we needed it. That's a miracle." *I hope it is.*

"Do you believe in miracles, Mom?"

"More and more every day, sweetie."

"I think my bad feelings just went away." She dozed off with a smile on her face as if angels were whispering in her ear.

§§§

The only thing faster than Luke Small's cruiser hurdling up Interstate Ninety Five to Bangor was his brain which was more like on an Olympic bobsled run. The events of the last two days were happening at light speed. Mr. Arnold MacDonald was not receptive to the search warrant on his properties. Shots were fired. Shots were returned. It took only a flesh wound for the mighty mountain man to toss out his guns and come out the front door with hands over his head. His white beard was blackened by fire, and he stunk, of smoke and other unidentified smells. Two gas cans, which apparently almost got him burned up, were rife with his fingerprints.

Charley Wickes got a heads up on the bat by Nate Munson, the evidence clerk. Mr. Munson was promptly fired. Charley Wickes never made it through the Jackman–Armstrong port of entry into Quebec Province and was being held by Canadian Custom authorities. They don't mess around.

Mack didn't do such a good job burying Susan's car. It was under the larger mound that looked like there was a car underneath. In the excavation, bones were found. The Coroner said they were bones of a teenage male. Todd Everett was pretty sure that the cold murder case of his boyhood friend was about to heat up. Mack would be trading his hermitage for a commune of likeminded souls with even more severe anti-social issues.

Jerry Moss called Todd Everett about that plea deal for Kevin Cook to which he replied, "What plea deal?" Jerry started preparing for trial. He would at least have his day of fame in court, even if only for a couple days. And it looked like he had two more clients. Things were looking up.

That was a lot of periods for Detective Small to put on his open cases in his short tenure. Chief Sullivan already had his retirement announcement pre-prepared. He would bow and exit stage left with what pride he had left. He recommended Luke Small as his replacement. The station did a poor job hiding their elation.

Luke pulled into Bangor International Airport short term parking. He walked into the terminal and waited in baggage claim with a cardboard sign that had one name on it: Perry Richardson. His flight had just landed.

Perry approached him with a smile upon seeing his name. "Detective Small? I am so pleased to meet you."

"Pleased to meet you," said the detective. "How was your flight?"

"Right on time," he replied. "Love to fly out of Palm Beach."

"Let's take a ride to Les Enfants. We can talk in the car."

Luke pulled out on to Union Street and headed east.

"Thank you so much for what you've done," said Perry.

"Well, you might want to hold your praise until I tell you what happened over the weekend. I could have filled you in over the phone, but I thought it would be best for you to hear it from me in person."

"What happened?" asked Perry.

"Things happened very fast over this weekend. We had a very close call, a fire. First of all, let me assure you Carl is OK. By that I mean . . . when I say he only ended up with a broken leg, take my word for it, that's a good thing. It was arson. Attempted homicide."

"What?" asked Perry staring at his driver with astonishment. "Who would want to kill him? Why?"

"His stepfather, Perry. Carl will be a hostile witness against him in his murder trial."

"I thought he was in jail."

"He is. But he had two accomplices. They were arrested this weekend. Carl is safe now. Nevertheless, I let Carl down. I promised to keep him safe. He wanted to stay in his house. I knew it would be difficult. I had routine patrols go by there every hour at night. They figured out the pattern."

"I'm sure you did everything thing possible, Luke," said Perry. "You have gone well above and beyond. I'm very grateful and thankful that he is OK. Where is he now?"

"He's staying with his uncle. David McKinley."

"David?" asked Perry. "Really?"

"You sound surprised," said Luke.

"It's interesting. He always seemed to have issues, but he's not a bad guy. I'm glad to see David stepping up. It makes me feel much better."

"Well, a lot of things are changing. Wait and see," said Luke. "You might see a different person."

Perry processed all this new information in silence for the rest of the short trip. Luke pulled into Les Enfants and parked. The two of them walked into the lobby wondering what the mystery meeting would reveal.

Nathan Bourassa came out to greet them. Each introduced themselves. "Well, it is so nice to finally meet all of you. I've never seen so many warrants, so much interest from so many people at one time for an adoption, actually two adoptions. I think you are going to be glad you came. Come on back to the conference room. There is someone I would like you to meet. I think the last piece of the puzzle."

Piece of the puzzle? wondered Luke. *Can this get any stranger?*

Henry Campbell sat alone fidgeting as the emotionless walls staring at him made him more nervous. Henry was a potato farmer from the County, as they called it, Aroostook County. Two hundred acres. Five generations and an earthy face to back it up. All of which would become meaningless if he were to lose his daughter. As the four men walked in, he stood up in his old suit with hand extended.

"Howdy. My name is Henry Campbell."

Nathan introduced each, but their names made no connection to Henry.

"Let me remove the confusion," said Nathan looking at Henry. "These two have both made inquiries into the adoption of a boy and a girl, twins, whose birth mother was Deborah McKinley. They know where the boy is. Carl Cook lives in Woodspring, Maine. They are still searching for the girl. The adoptive parents of the girl are Henry and his wife. They wanted to keep that information sealed. That was because they were concerned of interference if the birth parents should show up looking for her later remorseful for having let her out for adoption. Things have changed. Their daughter's name is Zoey. They now wish to unseal that information. I will let Henry explain why. But first, Maybe it would be good if each of you were to explain your interest in the twins. Perry, you had the first warrant issued. Maybe we can start with you?"

"Of course. Deborah was my wife. She is the birth mother of the twins. She passed recently and it was only then that I discovered that she had given birth in college to a set of twins and had them adopted. Carl and Zoey have a half brother and sister, also twins. I hope that it will be possible for them to be part of each other's lives."

"Luke? You also had a warrant issued."

"I'm the detective investigating the murder of Carl's adoptive mother, Susan Cook. As our investigation unfolded, we found out that Carl was unaware that he was adopted. So, we have pursued this in the course of the investigation in case there might be leads to follow."

"OK, Henry. Now you know everyone's involvement. You have their attention. Go ahead and explain your situation."

"I'll admit," started Henry, "that our motives are selfish."

"They're good selfish motives," interjected Nathan.

"I just don't want to come to you under any false pretenses," he said, his face running almost purple with emotion. "I'll get right to the point. I come hat in hand. Zoey, my daughter, has leukemia. She has had two bone marrow transplants. The first did not begin to work. Through Nathan, we contacted Deborah. She came to St. Jude's in Memphis about a year ago as a donor. It looked like it was going to work. Zoey was in remission." Then his face hit the floor as his voice started to crack. "After almost a year, we were hopeful. But now . . . she's worse off. Time is running out. We are looking for Carl, or her birth father, someone to save our baby."

Nathan put his hand on Henry's shoulder.

"Of course," said Perry. "She also has a half-brother and a half-sister. They might be matches."

"Carl would not hesitate, Henry," said Luke. "He'll be the first in line."

Henry looked up as though maybe the sun was finally starting to rise on the dark horizon. "Thank you."

"How soon does this procedure need to be done?" asked Perry.

"Quickly. There isn't much time," said Henry. "The doctor has told us privately that without a successful donor . . . well . . . he wouldn't commit. It has to be done soon."

"We would need for Carl to be tested," said Henry.

"I have a complete work up on Carl," said Luke. "We needed to do it as part of the investigation. If you have a fax number, I can have it sent to the doctor."

Henry pulled a card out of his jacket pocket. Luke called Sarah.

§§§

Henry had called Nancy and filled her in on the good news. His mouth went so fast, she had to make him stop and repeat it more than once in English. He told her about Perry Richardson, and Luke Small. The most promising match was Carl. Detective Small had already gotten a yes from Carl on the phone. He could be in Memphis at any time. They already had his blood work, DNA, etc. on file and faxed it to Dr. David to review for a match. She was to call him immediately when she got the results. He also told her that all of the above wanted to meet Zoey at some point in the future and not to worry. Like Deborah, these were giving people who would never take away what they had with their daughter, Zoey. They would only make it richer.

Zoey could almost levitate herself to the ceiling with excitement. "I can't wait," she said.

Nancy waited beside Zoey. It seemed like she was stuck in time. She was positive the hands on the clock were not moving. She kept sticking her head out in the hallway like a cuckoo clock canary. Finally, she could see Dr. David turn the corner with some papers. She prayed a small prayer. Her stomach twisted in anticipation of hearing the worst. *I do believe in miracles. I do.*

Her eyes screamed out the question before he was within hearing distance. She met him at the door.

Dr. David could no longer hold that tight professional facade. He broke into a smile. "It looks very promising. Very promising. When can he be here?"

XXIX

ZOEY CAMPBELL was moved to a large private room. She had no idea how that happened since her family had no financial means beyond what St. Jude's normally provided. Nancy, Zoey's perpetual sentinel and protector, was ready to wear out a new chair if necessary. It was Christmas Eve day. The best she could do was find a small plastic Christmas tree from the hospital gift store but that in no way lessened the gleam on Zoey's face as she decorated it with some colored lights and ornaments made out of construction paper. She was still weak, but her fever had subsided and the doctor said she would be ready for the procedure.

Henry walked through the door. "Hi, sweetie."

"Hi, Daddy," she said.

"I've got someone here I think you are going to want to meet."

Zoey raised the head of her bed and strained to see out the door. She loved surprises. "Who?"

A newly bald headed Carl stood in the doorway complete with leg cast, crutches, and a bandaged arm.

"Hi," he said and just stood there looking at her.

Zoey stared back, looking him up one side and down the other. "You look familiar. I know who you are," she said as her eyes watered. "I've always known you."

"I've known you too," he said as he hobbled over toward her bed.

"My goodness," she said. "What a mess you are. And you're going to save my life?"

"We're a pair," he laughed to staunch the tide of tears at the ready. "Yes. That is exactly what I'm going to do." He sat down in the chair on the side opposite Nancy.

"Nice to finally meet you," she said as she put out her hand.

Carl held her hand. It was warm and soft. "Nice to meet you too." She kept a firm grip on Carl's hand.

They sat quietly together as if catching up on a symbiotic relationship. Or they didn't know what to say. Nancy nodded to Henry. They slipped unnoticed out of the room and closed the door.

Finally Carl broke the silence. "So, tell me about yourself. Where have you been? Where do you live?"

"Not far," she said. "We have a farm. It's up north."

Carl smiled. "I thought I lived up north."

"There are those, even in Maine, who think the world ends at Bangor," she chuckled weakly. "But there is life north of that. You take Interstate Ninety Five to the end, turn left and keep going another hour."

"Wow. I live in Woodspring. Ever hear of it?"

She shook her head.

"Not missing much there either. Mostly woods. Moose. I like it though. So are you going to be a farmer?"

"No. Engineer. They say good engineers need a little farmer in them. What about you?"

"Writer. I'm going to be a writer. Novels, I think. My uncle, our uncle, is an author. He's going to teach me what he knows."

"Wow. That sounds exciting."

Carl nodded. He sat there for a few minutes trying to think of something else to say.

"I have a girlfriend," he blurted out and then his ears turned red. "Do you have a boyfriend?"

"Hmmm . . . not too many takers at the moment," she laughed. "I think they must be waiting for me to come out in some debutante ball. I want to know about your girlfriend. Tell me all about her."

Carl blushed. "Well, I think she's beautiful, smart, funny. Kind of like you."

"Sure," she said. "What happened to your leg?"

"Long story," he replied. "I jumped out of a two story window. This is what usually happens."

"Why would you do that?"

"When your house is on fire and it's the only way out, it's a pretty short decision."

"Oh, my goodness . . ."

Dr. David opened the door. "Ready, Carl?"

"Ready," he said. "Got to go. I'll see you soon. I'll be back tonight after this is over. We'll talk more."

§§§

When Zoey woke up, only Carl was in the room. He had his head back in the chair resting his eyes.

"What time is it?" she asked. The nurses had decorated the rooms and the nurses' station. She could see them pouring themselves a toast.

Carl looked at the clock. "Just after midnight. Merry Christmas."

"Merry Christmas," she returned. "Where is everybody? Mom?"

"They are resting in the hotel for the big day tomorrow. I'm taking care of you tonight."

"Well, thank you. How are you feeling?"

"Oh, I'm feeling fine. Just a little sore. The question is how are you feeling? Seems like they were in a rush to do this procedure."

"I'm about the same. It will take a few weeks before they know if it works."

"It will work," Carl said.

"I believe you. What's that?" she asked.

"My mother's Bible. I've been reading all the things she highlighted. There are a lot of them."

"Do you have a favorite?"

"I think I do. It's why I'm sure everything is going to work out like it's supposed to."

"Do you want to share it with me?"

"I do. But I'm not completely sure what it means yet. Let me work on it a while."

"You mean pray about it?"

"Something like that," he replied.

"I do that a lot," she said. "You said you were going to tell me about the fire."

"I'll have to go back to the beginning," he said and sadly relayed the story of his mother's murder, the investigation, how there was an attempt on his life, but he was safe now. All of them are in jail.

Zoey could feel a jab of pain with each episode he recounted as if she had been there with him when it was all happening. She reached out and took his hand once more.

"I'm so sorry. I had no idea. Tell me about your mother. What was she like?"

Carl looked up into heaven as if waiting for her to come down and show herself. "Well, she was my mother," he said, "my real mother. She was sweet, giving, generous. There was nothing she wouldn't do for me. Her life was for others."

"It sounds like she gave her life to save yours."

"She did. So, you met Deborah, our birth mother. I won't have that chance. Tell me about her."

"I think you just described her," she replied. Her face had a pleasant look as if she were replaying fond memories of their short time together.

"I guess what I don't understand is why would she not want us?"

"It's complicated. She gave me a letter. She had written long ago and waited for the right time. It was her way of saying she was sorry. It was a time when options seemed limited. She didn't make excuses. You could see the pain on her face, how she wanted to hold us, love us. But once the decision was made, she decided to bear the burden of that guilt alone. She tried to make sure we were well taken care of. In my case, that worked out well. She wanted my, our, forgiveness. It was easy to do. It was more difficult for her to forgive herself, but I think she did before she died."

"I'll have to ponder that," said Carl.

"You mean pray about it? Along with your favorite verse? Yet to be disclosed?"

"Yes."

The cot stayed cold that night. Carl fell asleep in his chair still holding Zoey's hand.

XXX

"**MERRRYYY CHRISTMAS,**" came a chorus of cheery voices from the doorway with two breakfast trays. They flipped on lights. "Rise and shine." The entire staff was going room to room decked out in Santa Claus outfits, Mrs. Claus, elves, and even reindeer. The entire floor was flooded with the sounds of laughing children.

Carl's and Zoey's eyes had little time to adjust.

"Merry Christmas again," said Carl.

"Merry Christmas."

They both wasted no time starting with the Christmas cookies first.

"Hungry?" she asked.

"Famished," he said slowing down. "Sorry. I'm an animal."

"I'm not one to talk. I'm ravenous. I feel so much better today and I don't know why. Maybe it's already working," she said. "We'll be famous. They'll write us up in the medical journals. Miracle twins!"

"I believe it is," he said. His sister emanated so much positive energy that he felt that if he could harness it he could fly around the room.

"I wonder where Mom and Dad are. They are usually here for breakfast."

She no sooner finished her words then they suddenly appeared as if she had wished it and it was so. Carl wouldn't have doubted.

"Merry Christmas, sweetie, Carl." Nancy kissed her girl and then Carl. "This is going to be the best Christmas ever."

Zoey looked at her like she had seen better. "Merry Christmas, Mom, Dad. I'm sure it will be."

Henry walked back to the door and peered down the hall. "We have some more people for you to meet this morning," he said.

"More? Mom, who do we know in Memphis?"

Carl looked around waiting for these others to appear out of thin air.

He looked again and there stood two giggly children on each side of a tall handsome man he had never seen before.

"Hi, I'm Jess. I'm your brother."

"Hi, I'm Bess. I'm your sister," she echoed.

Carl had a clue of who they were. Zoey had turned and was sitting up on the side of the bed now wondering if this were a dream.

Perry bent over and whispered something in their ears. "Well, guys. Go give your brother and sister a hug."

The eight year olds ran to Carl and Zoey as eight year olds can, while Carl braced for the impact. Jess and Bess zeroed in on their intended targets and then traded off.

Zoey leaned down and said. "Pleased to meet you. I'm Zoey. Your sister."

"And I'm Carl, your brother."

"We didn't mean to blindside you," said Perry. "I'm Perry. I was Deborah's husband. We just thought there couldn't be a better time to unite everyone together." Perry waked over and shook Carl's hand and kissed Zoey on the cheek. "I'm so glad to finally meet you both."

"Wow," said Carl. "I can't believe it. You came all the way to Memphis to spend Christmas."

"They are so adorable," said Zoey to which Jess took as an affront.

"We're not done," said Henry.

"Not done?" echoed Zoey. "What else could there be?" She had the two young ones sit on each side of her on the bed. "Could this get any better?"

"Oh, yes. It can get better," said Henry.

In walked David and Mary. "Hi. We're your aunt and uncle," said Mary walking over with no hesitation and giving Zoey and Carl big hugs. "I'm Mary."

David came over and gave Zoey a hug. "I'm David McKinley, Deborah's brother," he said.

Zoey looked at David, Mary, Carl, Jess, Bess, Bob, and Perry. "What a Christmas," she cried. "You were right. This is the best Christmas ever!"

"But there's still more," said Perry who orchestrated the event.

In walked Kathy, Luke, and Eva.

That was too much for Carl. "Kathy! This is who I was telling you about, Zoey," he said, the floodgates now open and rushing over as well as an invalid could and giving her a kiss. "This is Kathy and this is Luke and Eva. They're my surrogate Mom and Dad."

Kathy took pause at Carl's new hairdo.

Carl feigned smoothing hair with his hand. "Like it?"

She looked over at Zoey. Then at Carl. "Love it," she laughed walking over and kissing his bald head.

"Is there anymore?" asked Carl looking at Perry.

"That's it," said Perry.

The hospital staff started pulling chairs in. A coffee pot was placed on the table with more cookies and cupcakes decorated in festive colors. "What visitor policy?" they said as they all peered into the room to share in their joy.

They all surrounded Carl and Zoey as if afraid to lose them again. The chatter and laughter filled the hallways. So much to say. So many to say it. The conversations cris crossed any number of ways. Zoey placed Jess and Bess beside her. Kathy was joined to Carl. "What about the presents?" asked Jess.

"Presents?" asked Carl.

§§§

Perry reached out in the hallway and pulled in some bags. Perry handed Jess and Bess each a small present. They couldn't contain themselves as they walked over to Carl and Zoey. Inside were pictures of Deborah and Jess and Bess over the years.

"For the years we missed having you in our lives," said Perry.

"Thank you," they said.

"No, thank you," said Perry, "for letting us be here."

Sniffling seemed to become the most predominate sound as time went on.

"What about the rest of you?" asked Carl. "We can't be the only one with presents."

"Oh, we already have our presents," said David. "We have you in our lives. We have the gift of life," he said tearing up and taking Mary's hand. "Thanks to Deborah and Perry. The Bible, which I have been reading a lot more lately, says greater love has no one than this, that someone lay down his life for his friends."

"And I can say the same thing," said Zoey. "Thank you, Carl. I know that you just gave me the gift of life. What more can one give?"

"And how could we be any more thankful, Carl. Thank you for giving us hope, and love," said Henry.

"Well, I do know someone else who has a present to give," said Kathy looking over at her Dad. "He feels a little awkward doing it here, but Christmas was the day he promised me."

Luke turned on one knee to Eva who looked as if suddenly there was no one in the room but the two of them. "Yes," she cried before he opened the little box.

The clapping drew people from the nurses' station to see what the commotion was.

"Well, there is one more thing," said Perry as he pulled one more item out of the bag.

Everyone looked around wondering if this was the bag that Jesus used to feed the five thousand.

He handed it to Carl. It was addressed to My Darling Son. Carl looked over at Zoey.

"I got mine in person, Carl," she said as she tried to hold back tears so he could read it.

"You don't have to read it now, Carl," said Perry.

"No, I want to." He opened the envelope. There was a picture of Deborah with two newborns, one in each arm. It was haunting, filled with a mix of such joy conjoined with regret. He put it back in the envelope and pulled out the letter. As he read, it got so quiet the nurses checked to make sure everyone in the room hadn't flat lined. His new family watched as his face went through several iterations finally ending with a peaceful look. He smiled and nodded and was quiet for a couple more minutes as if in prayer.

Carl looked around the silent room. All eyes were on him. He pulled out his mother's Bible and looked over at Zoey as if to say this is it.

"I can't possibly explain how this day came to be. How so many people crossed paths in Memphis, Tennessee. I do know we can sum it up with one word. Love. It fills this room.

My mother had many verses highlighted. Let me read this one from First Corinthians Thirteen:

Love is patient and kind; love does not envy or boast; it is not arrogant or rude. It does not insist on its own way; it is not irritable or resentful; it does not rejoice at wrongdoing, but rejoices with the truth. Love bears all things, believes all things, hopes all things, endures all things.

"That describes both my mothers. That describes the people in this room. I went through a very dark period in my life. I felt like I was unloved. That no one wanted me. That God had abandoned me. It was all about me. All I could see was darkness, but it was a delusion. I wasn't seeing the light that was always there. This is my mother's favorite verse from Matthew Six:

The light of the body is the eye: if therefore thine eye be single, thy whole body shall be full of light.

"Now I understand what she meant. God was there all the time. Working His love in us no matter how dark it seemed, even in all the tragedy we have seen. The light was always there. We just needed eyes that see. She called it having the seeing eye. The proof of her faith is gathered around us here today. Thank all of you for coming into my life." And he closed the book.

"And God bless us, everyone," chorused Jess and Bess.
To which they all said in unison, "Amen."

ACKNOWLEDGEMENTS

A special thanks to Don Cogswell for his assistance in the cover design.

CPSIA information can be obtained
at www.ICGtesting.com
Printed in the USA
FFOW02n1211240618
47193930-49912FF

9 781732 310902